GLITCHED AWAY

GLITCHED AWAY

By Ronald Knipfer

Self-Published with help from

MIDNIGHT EXPRESS BOOKS

GLITCHED AWAY

Copyright © 2014 by Ronald Knipfer

ISBN-13: 978-0692419885 (Midnight Express Books)
ISBN-10: 0692419888

Self-Published with help from
MIDNIGHT EXPRESS BOOKS
POBox 69
Berryville AR 72616
(870) 210-3772
MEBooks1@yahoo.com

GLITCHED AWAY

By Ronald Knipfer

ACKNOWLEDGEMENTS

I would like to thank the people who created the Morrowind Series also known as the Elder Scrolls. I would like to thank the people who played the games with me, and I would like to make sure that the people who inspired me to write these stories that their input was well-received.

INTRODUCTION

I was playing a video game called Oblivion, when a thunderstorm began forming outside my house out in the country. At the time, I didn't think I had much to worry about, as I had battery back-up with a power- surge strip. The thing was; it wasn't strong enough to compensate for the lightening strike that I got. Lightening struck my fuse box outside my house and sent a surge of unrelenting electricity through my battery back-up, then through my surge protector and up my leg.

I woke up in a prison cell. When I gathered my wits and the fog had cleared, I looked around and it was all very strange. I was in a stone and mortar cell with a steel cage for a door. I looked down at myself and I was wearing rags. I did not know where I was or how I got here. Also as the fog cleared I noticed that off in the distance everywhere I looked there was a small diamond floating in the air in front of me. No matter where I turned, there it was.

As I moved around my cell - a 6' X 8' mass or mortar and stone - at first, I could not recall where I was the night before and what I was doing for the likes of me. Then it hit me, I was playing Oblivion. It was an epiphany. I looked around the Stone cell, and this was just like the stone cells in the game. I had seen them so many times. I had rescued NPC's many, many times. This must be some kind of nightmare. I slapped my face several times, cried out, "Somebody help me!" and no one came.

This was magic pure and simple. Somehow, I was in the video game. I had played the game so many times as so many different characters, now I have to play it for real. This was going to be some adventure. Some people get all the luck don't they?

I moved to the gate of the cell, looked around. I looked to see if anyone was walking the hallways. I listened for voices. This just might be the part of the game where the Royal party comes through the jail cells. How long was I going to have to wait? There is an elf in the cell across from mine. "Hey, elf!" I yelled, "Wake up!" He came to his door.

"I told him with all the determination that I had, that I was going to make a break for it when the Royal Party came through and that he was welcome to make a break with me if he wanted to. He said back to me, "You are going to die, that is all you are going to do." He continued to taunt me for a few minutes and then the sound of keys jingling began to echo down the corridor, and then he shut up.

Glenroy, Barus, and Captain Renault were escorting Emperor Uriel Septim VII through the jail. Captain Renault told me to stand aside as she approached my cell. After she opened the door, she shoved my bunk to one side and pushed on the wall, and a door appeared in the wall.

Playing the game, I knew that this cell was supposed to be empty. This was it, I was in the game. I was in for the fight of my life. If this was some kind of dream only time would tell if I was going to wake up. Maybe I lay in some hospital in a coma. Let's hope I've played the game enough that I will be able to stay alive for awhile.

The only move I had to make was to follow the Royal Party through the passageway. I kept to the shadows as I moved along the corridor. An ambush lay ahead. The Royal Party was going to be attacked by a few men in dark robes. I watched from my corner in the shadows - as I had no weapon to help anyone - in awesome horror. When it was over, Captain Renault lay dead on the floor and next to her there was a sword, the Akaviri Katana along with a torch. I picked up the sword and hefted its weight in my hand. It was a rather light sword about 2 feet in length. I thought that I may be able to handle it well. I slid it in the belt around my waist. The Sword does at least 24 points of damage.

As played in the game, I inspected the bodies of the dead; I found 4 bottles of healing potion. I picked them up and stuffed them in my shirt and looked for the Royal Party and saw a door closing. I knew the door to be locked, and that there was a hole in the wall to the South, so I made my way there. I stuck my head in and found a large rat about the size of a cat or even a raccoon sitting on a chest. I stuck to the wall as I made my way, I didn't want to draw the rat's attention. It might be good practice, but I wasn't ready yet. I needed to find a change of clothes first. Something more fit for this world. Even with all the fancy costumes available in this world, the rags that I was wearing just would not do in this land of magic and sorcery; I needed something that would afford me some protection against all of the hostile creatures of this land.

As I made my way, I came across a skeleton that had an Iron Dagger, a Leather Cuirass and Boots. There were also 28 Iron Arrows, 6 picks and a Torch. Nearby there was also a Leather Shield, an Iron Bow and a small chest with a Sapphire Gem and 10 gold pieces. Near the chest was a sack with 4 gold pieces, a pick, a Rabbit pelt and a necklace, 2 silver nuggets and a wedge of cheese.

I put on the Cuirass and the Boots. I put the bow across my back and the quiver that now full held 30 arrows. I stuffed everything in the sack that would fit. I continued looking around the room, in the corner was another chest, this one containing: a Rusty War Axe and 6 Gold pieces. Near the chest was a crate that contained: 2 clubs, 4 torches, 4 picks, an Iron Dagger, and 12 Iron Arrows. Just down the wall is a dead Goblin with 3 scrolls one of which was a fire damage spell, and the other 2 were Chameleon spells; there was also a restore magic potion on him. Near the corpse lay 3 more picks and an iron key.

I took the time to lay everything out. I could only carry so much weight and only had 4 pockets. The sack might be able to hold a little weight. It was made out of some canvas type material which is sturdy until it dry rots. I had 20 gold pieces, a Sapphire Gem and 2 silver nuggets which were enough to buy various supplies when I came across a store. I knew that I could sell the Rabbit pelt and the necklace as well. There were 10 picks; I pulled the ones that were in the best shape which meant tossing 4 of them. I decided the best weapon for me at this point and time until I became a better fighter is the bow, so I tossed the clubs and the War Axe and the Dagger. I tossed 3 of the torches. The leather shield got tossed. This left me with the fire damage spell, 2 Chameleon spells, and a restore magic potion, 4 Healing potions, the wedge of cheese and the Iron key.

The door ahead of me was locked, I tried the key that I found and it worked. When I opened the door, there were a lot of rats. There must have been about a dozen. I stood at the door and picked them off one at a time, it took me a while, several of them even came at me and I had to stab them with the arrow instead of shooting it. The diamond that is floating in the air provided me with a way to find my targets a lot easier. I knew right away that using a bow in this land was going to be my weapon of choice. It took me a few minutes to get used to using the diamond, and after I was able to use it, killing the rats became easy. It took all of the arrows, there was no need for me to go and retrieve any of the arrows after the attack was over. I took the time to skin a couple of the larger rats to take the meat for eating later. A chest lay in the room and it contained nothing I could carry except for a healing potion. There was an Iron Cuirass, Iron greaves, 24 more arrows, 5 picks, 3 torches, another Iron Bow, and a war axe.

I continued down the corridor to the east, there was a bend in the corridor to the north. As I moved on there were five rats attacking what looked like a zombie, I took out the rats so I could take on the zombie. I turned another corner which was going east. Another room and another chest. This time I found twenty gold pieces three more picks and two more torches. I picked up the gold pieces and the sack was getting pretty heavy to carry by now.

I soon found myself on an upper ledge, looking down and seeing no way to go except down climbing down. I looked around for a rope and finding none, the only way down was to scale the wall. I tossed the bow and the quiver and the sack over the edge so they would not interfere with my attempt to scale the wall. I made it about fifteen minutes later. I continued going north, and this led me to a large room with another chest and a pile of loot and an Iron War Hammer, an Iron Shield, an Iron Helmet, some lettuce, two wedges of cheese, and a tomato. Continuing on north then west I came across a sack with a healing potion. I drank the healing potion, hoping that it would help, I haven't been wounded yet but I am getting tired. It did help a little; it isn't like restorative magic that can invigorate my muscles, which is what I need.

I hoped to find an end to this soon, I was finding a lot of stuff, and I couldn't carry too much more. The arrows were definitely a burden on me. I consider myself to be a healthy individual of good stock. I'm almost 6 foot. I weigh in at 180 and built pretty solid. I can carry what I have and carry it well; I just don't have a good bag to carry a lot of the items that I am finding. I'd like to find an end to this tunnel and be able to create a pile of all of these items and then find a market and make a couple of trips to someone who will buy my finds from me and this way until I find my way back home, I will be able to take care of myself. I kept the sack in case I find other small items that I can carry.

I know what lay ahead of me, and until I find my way back home, this journey is going to be a perilous one. This world is fraught full of monsters and evil men, there are bandits, pirates, assassins, and goons of every shape and size. There are goblins, and elves, and ogres, and dragons, and other monsters that I will have to learn to fight and battle for my life. This isn't going to be like playing the game either, death and reset, I am sure if I get killed it will be the end of me.

Playing the game out, I wonder, when I accomplish tasks in the game and earn level ups, how is that going to affect me in here. Like walking around and jumping about, after awhile in playing the game, the fatigue meter gets longer. The more I use the repair hammer, the greater my skills become. Making potions, the more potions that I attempt to make or do make, the greater my skills become. The more magic I use the more powerful I become; will all of this and more happen to me as well? These advancements in the game mean leveling up every so often. What if anything will happen to me? It is going to be interesting to find out.

So far it has only been the rats and the one Zombie. At the end of this tunnel that I am trekking through there will be several goblins. I am sure of it.

Further west there was a barrel, with four potions of Ale, one down the gullet, and what do you know there was a Restore Fatigue Potion as well. The tunnel turned south and became a winding tunnel. I came to a room with Wisp Stalk Plants and Cairn Bolete Mushrooms and a wedge of cheese. Continuing on, there were 50 Stinkhorn Caps and a natural cavern that looked to contain a booby trap alarm system.

Creeping up, I found a patrol goblin, I looked for and found a crevice in the wall, and cocked an arrow into the bow and caught my breath and as I exhaled I let the arrow fly right into the goblin's neck and down he went without a sound. I remembered this to be a goblin hideout so I crept around the corner and there was another goblin and again, another breath and another arrow right in the skull, down and out, I crept up to him and dragged him back to the other one and set his body next to the other one.

So far so good; lady luck was with me. Two goblins - two arrows and two quick deaths. So far, better than what I could have hoped for.

Sneaking around the first part of the cave I came across a crate that was being used as a table. There was a chest in a nook to the north that held twenty gold pieces.

Moving along, there was a trip wire and just on the other side of the wire was a goblin. I rushed the wire and dove just as three maces came crashing down from the ceiling and smashed the ugly creature.

Persevering south I found a campfire. On the east wall I came to an opening and took a look around the corner. A Goblin sitting on a chest facing my way. I prayed that lady luck would be with me again. I cocked another arrow and inhaled and exhaled and as I let the arrow fly it hit the goblin right in the chest and he fell over dead.

I scampered across the opening in the wall and resumed down the tunnel. The tunnel sloped downward and I spotted two goblins off in the distance, I thought to take them both out this close to each other I am going to have to have some help. Then I remembered there is a rolling log trap in this hallway. I should be coming up on it any moment. I'll just set the trap off and let it kill the goblins.

Oh well, that's two more down and a handful to go.

At the end of the corridor was a small room, with several goblins in it and a Goblin Witch was off to the right. This was going to be a little bit harder. I crept around to a dark corner, and pulled out a Chameleon Scroll, and read the words aloud, but just loud enough that no one but the spirits of magic could hear me. I sure hope this works.

I slotted another arrow aiming for the closest goblin and let loose. A hit but it didn't kill him. I had to hit him again. He took off running and hitting a target on the run, not sure I could do that; a chance I had to take. I gave it my best shot and hit him in the back. Then quickly slotting another I hit the goblin on the chest in the face. This left the Witch that was in the corner. She was sitting up straight muttering something I was sure she was trying to either expose me or create some kind of protection spell. It took three arrows for me to kill her.

The room exited to the northeast. I set everything down in the middle of the room and ran back to the beginning and started opening chests and crates and hauling everything to the center of the room. It took me several trips to make sure I had everything. As this was end of the tunnel, I need to make sure that I had everything that I could carry was valuable. There is no coming back.

All total I collected: bottles of ale (4), Chameleon spell (1), daggers (2), fire damage spell (1), Flawed gems (2), Flawed ruby, Gold nugget (1), Gold pieces (60), Healing potions (7), Iron arrows (60), Iron Helmet, Iron long sword, Iron Shield, Iron War Hammer, lettuce, Magical Shaman staff, Mortar and pestle, Necklace, Petty soul gem, picks (18), Rabbit pelt, Rat portions (20), Repair hammers (2), Restore fatigue potion, restore magic potion, Sapphire Gem (1), Silver (2), Silver vase (1), Stinkhorn Caps, Iron key (1), tomato (1), torches (2), wedges of cheese (2), Wisp Stalk Caps,

The quiver only held 30 arrows and that was all I could carry for Iron, using the chest in the corner, I put everything that I couldn't take with me in it. This meant leaving behind: Iron arrows (30), Iron Helmet, Iron long sword, Iron Shield, Iron War Hammer, Silver vase (1), torches (2), and daggers (2). I drank 2 of the ale and left 2. I drank I one the Restore fatigue potion and left 1. The Stinkhorn Caps (50) and the Wisp Stalk Caps (50).

I kept the Chameleon spell (1), the fire damage spell (1), Gold pieces (60), the lettuce, the Magical Shaman staff, the Necklace, the Rabbit pelt, the Rat portions (20), the Sapphire Gem (1), the Iron key (1), the tomato (1), and the wedges of cheese (2), Healing potions (7), Repair hammers (2) picks (18), Gold nugget (1), Flawed gems (2), Flawed ruby, the Mortar and pestle, the Petty soul gem, the restore magic potion, and Silver (2), and I still held the sword: the Akaviri Katana.

As I exited the tunnel, I saw the Royal Party, the Emperor asked me to join them so I did. Then the Emperor began talking to me in the tongue of this strange and foreign land. So I nodded my head every so often. Then the assassins returned. I pushed the Emperor behind me, and we backed up behind Glenroy, and Barus, as they battled the assassins. Then three more assassins came from behind us.

After the battle was over, the Party headed for the subterranean levels. Then Glenroy motioned for Barus, me and the Emperor to stay put while he checked out what was in front of us. About 10 minutes later he came back and told us to join him. We came to a gate that shouldn't have been locked, he said something about us going south and sure as shit, some more assassins came and Glenroy and Barus rushed off to deal with them.

The Emperor handed me an Amulet and by magic I was able to understand the language of this land. He told me to take the Amulet to his last heir Jauffre. The Amulet is called "The Amulet of the King" and I was to protect it with my life. As he finished speaking a Mythic Dawn assassin came out of the shadows and killed the king and as he was coming for me Barus returned and killed him.

When he turned to me, he saw the Amulet and told me that Jauffre was at the Weynon Priory and he told me about the sewers. He said to me, "Jauffre is the Grandmaster of the Blades" and lives as a simple monk in Weynon Priory." He then told me, "Go to the city of Chorrol which is southeast from here. When you get to the exit in the sewers just head straight west and you will come to the Priory."

Off I ran.

CHAPTER 1

MY JOURNEY BEGINS

I exited the sewers just northeast of Imperial City. I was on an island in the Northeast corner of Lake Rumare, which served as the Capitol's mote.

My first thoughts in no particular order were: What next? Where do I go? Who do I talk to? What do the fates have in store for me? Will I ever be able to find my way out of this world? Would I really want to?

To make sure that I meet my needs, the best that I could do right now, is to sell some of the stuff that I picked up. I put the Amulet of the King around my neck and was going to keep it there until I had found Jauffre at the Weynon Priory.

It was time to run to see Norbert Lelies at Lelles' Quality Merchandise to see how much I could talk him into giving me for this junk and trade. I need cash for clothing, weapons, and tools, and I also need to pay for training in skills. So I set off in a light jog in search of Lelles' Quality Merchandise.

Selling to Norbert, I talked him into taking from me: the Chameleon spell, the Fire Damage spell, the Magical Shaman staff, the Necklace, the Rabbit pelt, the twenty Rat portions, the Sapphire Gem, five of the Healing potions, fifteen of the picks, the Gold nugget, both of the

Flawed gems, the Flawed ruby, the Petty soul gem, the restore magic Potion, the two pieces of Silver.

My mercantile skills need a little work, I didn't get quite what I was hoping for, but it was a decent start I guess. He gave me a trade on some leather clothes and armor, and I got a better bow, and $2000 pieces of gold.

Next it was time to find someone who could direct me to the Thieves Guild. I went into town and found a beggar, gave him a gold piece worth $20.00 and this raised his disposition towards me and he was receptive to me asking him questions.

"Who are you?"

"Where am I at?"

"What is this place?"

"What are the people like?"

"Where is the best place to look for work?"

"You will want to join the Thieves Guild first, so you will need to go to the Garden of Dareloth in the Waterfront District and talk to Armand Christophe."

When I found Armand there were two other would be thieves talking to him, they were Methredhel and Amusei.

Armand told all three of us, "If you want a place in the Thieves Guild, you need to get me the diary of Amantius Allectus."

He continued on, "The only rule is that you couldn't kill each other or Allectus."

I noticed a beggar sleeping by the North wall on my way over here, so I ran back to him.

"Excuse me, sir, I need your assistance."

He woke with a yawn.

The beggar's name was Puny Ancus. "What can I do you for?"

"First I would like to give you $20.00 gold, and then I would like to ask you a couple of questions."

"Fine by me."

He put out his dirty hand, that hadn't been washed in days, and I handed him the gold.

"I'll tell you whatever it is that you want to know."

"I need to find a man that goes by the name of Allectus; can you tell me where I can find him?

"The man that you are looking for lives in Temple District's East End." He filled me in as the where and what.

I ran to the Temple District hoping that Methredhel and Amusei didn't have a clue as to how to find Allectus. I needed this job. I wouldn't kill to get it, but I would do just about anything else to make sure that I got it. When I got to the East gate, I turned south down the last lane just before the gate and when I got to the first door on my right, and picked the two tumbler locks and let myself in.

I rummaged through everything on the ground floor keeping my ears open for any sounds from above. I didn't have time to find out where this guy is and what he is doing, I needed this diary and I needed it now. As I searched through the desk, I found it. I ran out of the house and down the road. I stopped to catch my breath and to calm down after such an exhilarating turn of events. My adrenaline was pumping and I could hear my heart beating in my ears. As I sat there, I opened the diary and paged through it scanning its contents. Once I had calmed down, I ran back to Christophe and gave him the diary and I was accepted into the Thieves Guild.

"Alright the next job that I have for you is not that easy."

"I'll do whatever you ask me to do."

"Those are some powerful words that you are speaking there."

"I mean it Christophe, whatever you want me to do, and I'll do it."

"Okay then, since you said that, what I want you to do is to find a house, any house I don't care where it is, you just break into it, steal enough loot and then find a fence."

"I haven't had a lot of experience breaking into houses, but I can do it."

"The drawback here kid is that you need to steal enough and convince the fence to give you at least $2,850 gold without asking you any questions."

"It can't be that hard to find fence, can it?"

"It isn't as easy as you might think it is."

"Well, is there anything that you would be willing to say, to give me a tip?"

"The only clue that I will give you is that there is a fence in Burma named Ongar."

I walked around for a couple of hours checking out houses and the activity at different places. It took me a little while, the better part of the day I would say, and then I found one that was just right. I went into sneak mode and looked around and watched for people coming and going as I picked the lock on the front door and went inside.

I looked around for the most expensive looking items that were in the house. I picked up over what I thought had to be at least $5,000 worth of stuff and headed off to Burma to find Ongar.

When I got back to Christophe, I gave him the $3,000 gold that I got from Ongar and he smiled at me.

"You know kid, this is the fastest turnaround time that I have ever had anybody bring me the fee for the list of fences that I have. You did very well. You can feel proud of yourself."

"Well thanks Christophe. I really appreciate that."

"Don't thank me yet, the jobs are just beginning."

"All you have to do is ask, like I told ya before. I mean it, I need this and I will do whatever you ask."

"Just so you know; I've got a laundry list of stuff that needs to be done."

"Any time and any place."

"We'll take it one step at a time and see how you do on each job."

"Right now, here is a list of fences and a list of houses that need to be broken into. The fences in this land are very harsh at making deals, you are going to have to work on your mercantile skills if you ever hope to gain any favor from these guys."

"I'll catch up with you when this job is done."

"Don't go to jail. Whatever you do, don't go to jail."

"I won't. I promise you that I won't."

"Famous last words."

To be a successful thief, one has to have a knack at stealing, quick with the fingers, and quick with the feet. It takes a lot of brains to be able to steal from someone. Courage helps, it helps real well. The adrenaline rush is fantastic, it gives a boost. The hardest part is taking that adrenaline and using it the way a thief should. It takes calm, nerves of steel. The breathing must be even; the heart rate slow. The muscles in the arms and the legs need to be limber, if you plan to climb or to run. The best thieves always walk away from their hits.

Breaking into a home when you know that you can get caught, in broad daylight with the hustle and bustle of neighbors and other people walking by, well that takes nerves. The adrenaline that rushes through you, most amateur thieves don't use that adrenaline the right way and they usually wind up in the slammer.

Not me, I had a lot of practice in my previous life, and I was only going to get better in Cyrodiil. A land with a million houses just waiting for my nimble little fingers. There wasn't a police force to deal with like there was in the world where I came from. No automobiles, no cars of any kind; walking to and from every destination, makes life so much better.

So, you see I realize that I had become a part of the world of Cyrodiil, and this world has real magic, not stage magic. Magic here isn't about sleight of hand and being quicker than the eye, magicians aren't experts at distracting people from the illusion; magic in Cyrodiil is about power; real power—a power that comes from the soul.

Every soul in every life has been gifted with power; can you tap into that power? Can you learn how to use the power that you were born with?

Well, in Cyrodiil the best place to learn to how to do this is to take a stop at the Mage's Guild. The mages at the guild will teach you how to tap into the power that we are born with but it costs. Nothing in life is free, and the mage's have the patience to teach. Not many people have the required patience, and part of making your way through the guild is to learn patience because learning and casting spells takes time. You aren't going to learn a fireball spell, for example, and be able to cast it 100 times out of 100. It may take you 300 tries, maybe even 400 tries to cast it 100 times. Not until you build your faith in yourself and your power will you be able to cast 100 times out of 100.

Well, stopping at the Mage's Guild was going to be a priority. I needed to be able to learn some spells that would help me become the greatest thief in Cyrodiil.

My first stop on this quest was at the Mage's Guild to see if I could find a spell and buy it. I needed to fortify my strength so that I could carry more without overworking myself. There is one thing about this land, there are caves and dungeons everywhere with everything that you can imagine that have long been forgotten by the people that put them there or that have since died, and this stuff is just sitting there waiting for someone like me to come along and just help myself to it.

I went into the Mage's Guild and walked up to the first mage that I saw.

"I need some help. Do you think that you can help me?"

"We'll see, that depends."

"What does that mean?"

"What that means, is I may be willing to help you, but we all have different jobs here and depending on what you need, I may not be the one to help you, I may have to direct you somewhere else?"

"Okay, I read you."

"Now, what do you need?"

"I need to buy a spell that will increase my strength and ability to carry things."

"For that you need to go downstairs, just tell her that I sent you."

When I got downstairs, there was a female mage standing in the corner, contemplating the mysteries of the universe I presume. She looked deep in thought and the last thing that I wanted to do was to interrupt someone who might be on the verge of cracking another of life's mysteries.

I strode up to her with all the confidence that I could muster, and said, "Excuse me ma'am."

She looked down at me, "What can I do for you son?"

"The mage at the door said that you would be able to help me, and I sure hope that you can."

"Well what is it son?"

"I want to be an explorer in this fabulous land, and I need to be able to increase my strength so that when I go deep into the caves and caverns that I have heard about, I will be able to fill my bag with as much as it will carry. Can you help me with this spell?"

"I sure can young man. This first thing that I am going to do for you is to transform your bag into an inter-dimensional one that can carry every item that you want to carry no matter the size so if you were to, let's say, come across 100 swords, you would be able to put all of them in your bag and they would be there when you needed them."

With a wave of her hand, my bag transformed into the bag she described. My thought ran a million miles a second at the possibilities.

"My young friend, do you have $500 in gold?"

"Yes ma'am."

"Good."

I handed her the $500 gold.

She then taught me Fortify Strength and Soul Trap.

"This spell that you want is a permanent spell, it won't just affect what you can carry, it will affect everything that you do, so if you were to punch a wall, if your strength were up enough, you could knock down a wall."

"So, if I get into a fight with someone, I could hurt them if I am not careful."

"That is exactly what I am telling you."

"When you go to cast this on yourself even though the radius is directed at you, if someone or some animal were to inadvertently stumble into the spell you could affect them as well. So I need you to find a place, presumably outside of town and go into the woods and cast it.

I did what she told me to and I walked out of town in to the edge of the woods, and looked around, there were no animals, and it took me several tries to be able to cast the spell, as I had no magic skills. Then once I started casting, I failed several more times, all totaled I would say that it took me about 50 tries to cast it on myself 20 times. I brought strength up to 2,050.

To fulfill the job that Christophe gave me, the first house that I went to was Heinrich Oaken-Hull's Place in Anvil. The first thing that any good burglar does is scope out his victim. You just don't walk into the first house you see with guns blazing. You watch them, look for regular visitors, look for habits, watch for family, you watch sometimes a day, sometimes a week, sometimes even longer. I had to wait outside his house for several hours until he left.

After he left, I crept down to his place and picked his locks and looted his place for all that I could. I went back to Ongar and sold to him little more than half of what I thought that I could get. I sold the rest to others store owners for a small profit.

It took me several days to go down the list of houses that Christophe gave me. I was able to break into each house and steal something and then I went to each of the fences and worked on my mercantile skill getting to know each one so that later on when I needed them they would be there for me. To me, at the time, that seemed to be the most important part, getting to know them and making sure they knew me and that I would be fair with them and hoped that they would be fair with me.

I made my way back to Christophe and let him know that I had done the deed.

"It didn't take you long at all. It seems that you have a real flair for this sort of thing. You just might become head of the guild if you can keep this up."

"Do you have any jobs for me right now?"

"It just so happens that if you are ready to start knocking off items on my laundry list, we can get to it." "I'm ready."

"Your first quest is called "Untaxing the Poor". Find Hieronymus Lex and clean out his office."

CHAPTER 2

MY LIFE AS A THIEF BEGAN

I knew that I may never become a Wizard, but a magical thief, now that's a whole new ball game. A magical thief will throw a wrench in everyone's conceptions. Don't know if anyone in this land had ever encountered a magic using thief, but watch out Cyrodiil, here I come.

This Hieronymus Lex isn't going to know what hit him. Cleaning out the tax-collector's office, now, that seems like a job to do. If the guy is corrupt, and his office with all of his records is cleaned out, he will have to start over again. I liked the idea.

I had to go back to the Waterfront District and ask Puny Ancus for help. As usual he was sleeping as he had nothing else to do it seemed. I needed information on a guy who went by the name of Hieronymus Lex. Puny told me that Lex had an office in the South Watchtower near Allectus' house in the Temple District. His last words of advice, "You better watch out, breaking into some of these offices are booby trapped by different spells and that my boy can bring you a world of hurt."

It was time to go back to the mages guild.

I went back to the mage who sold me the fortify strength spell, and told her about what Puny told me and she worked with me and sold me a bunch of low-level spells and told me that there were plenty of places in the guild that I could practice my skills.

So I set out to test my skills. I found an empty room and began casting different spells and picking the locks. It wasn't easy at first. Then it dawned on me after several hours of trying this, I needed to learn to be able to detect the spells first. So, I had to go back and see if I could buy a detect spell from the mage. Sure enough, she had one and I bought it. It made life a little easier. Not a whole lot, but some.

I spent several hours honing my skills, and getting better at detecting spells and traps, and being able to pick locks that had them attached without setting them off. It began to boost my confidence and after a while, I thought that I had what it took to be able to successfully navigate the terrain and be a good "booster".

I ran back to the Temple District and found my way to the Southern Watchtower and walked up to see if Lex was in. It was the luckiest day of my life. Lex wasn't in. I climbed the ladder, sure enough, there was a spell on the lock, and I was able to successfully pick the lock on the trap door, and went inside. I walked over to his desk, and grabbed all of the gold and the tax records that were in the desk and got the heck out of there.

I carried all of the stuff back to Christophe and he told me, "You can keep all of the gold, I don't want it."

He then said to me, "You are now known as 'Footpad' I will notify all of the other guilds by messenger. If you want the job, there is a bust of the late Countess of Cheydinhal and I want it. Find Luckless Lucina, a beggar, and she will help you."

I figured what the hell. But it would be tomorrow. Right now, I needed a nap. I hadn't slept in over 30 hours and my bones were tired. I ached from head to toe. I really couldn't think all that straight. I went out into the woods and found a good spot and I took off my armor and laid down for a nap.

When I woke up, several hours later, I was hungry. There was a red screen in front of me. It was a level up screen; it offered me three choices to appoint areas for me to level up. Strength, Agility, Magic, Wisdom, Health, and Fortitude; each one had a varying amount of points for me to choose from but I could only pick from 3. The lettuce and the cheese and the tomato all went down the gullet. I was going to have to find an abandoned shack or something to claim as my own before the day was out though.

I headed off to Cheydinhal's West gate. I had to give Luckless Lucina a $20.00 gold piece for her to help me. She told me that the bust was in the Countess's guarded and haunted tomb in the undercroft of the Chapel of Arkay. When I got there I found a patrolling guard. So, I watched and waited and learned the timing of the guard. The bust was on the West side so when the guard went down the East side I ran in quick grabbed the bust and ran out before she could spot me.

I headed back to the Waterfront District with the bust in my bag, and when I got there, the place was full of guards, and Christophe was nowhere to be found. I walked around until I found Puny and asked him about Christophe, the only information he offered, "Methredhel is looking for you." I hung around until she showed up.

"What's up?"

"The theft of the bust was not an actual commissioned theft; it was the beginning of an elaborate plan to eliminate a mole inside the guild."

"Okay. Where does that leave me?"

"I have been told to tell you that you are to pin the theft on Myvrynra Arano."

"Sure. No problem."

"He lives here in the Waterfront District. Break into his home plant the bust and then go tell Lex that you heard that Arano has the bust. Can you do that?"

"Sure."

I broke into Arano's home and planted the bust in the cupboard. Walked over to the temple District and found Lex in his office, and asked him if I could talk to him. I had to pay him but I was able to boost his disposition in the process and we walked over to Arano's and I followed him in and sure enough the bust was where I put it and Arano was arrested.

I went back to the Garden and Christophe still wasn't around so I walked around looking for an abandoned shack or apartment, something that I could squat in and call my own. I found an old shack outside of town. There were spider webs, dust and dirt everywhere. It took me several hours to clean the place up. There was a pump house out back for me to wash up in after I woke up in the mornings. It would be cold but it was better than nothing.

After I cleaned the house, I had several hours to find something new and interesting. As I walked around town collecting all of the sights, I found an alchemist. I went into her store.

"Good afternoon, young man."

"Good afternoon ma'am."

"Is there something special that you are interested in?"

"To tell you the truth, I was thinking about becoming an alchemist."

"Well you have come to the right place."

"I don't know anything about it, I have heard that it is an interesting occupation."

"It is, we use every ingredient that nature has to offer us, so that nothing goes to waste"

"Everything?"

"Yes, everything."

"What do I need to get started?"

"You need to get a few basic supplies, the tools for mixing the ingredients, and scale for measuring them and the bottles to put your potions in."

"I've $3,000 gold to give you is this enough to get me started?"

"It is."

So, I gave the nice young lady, the $3,000 gold and she gave me everything that I needed and I walked home with the alchemy set and set up shop.

I decided that I should spend the next few days going out and collecting all kinds of herbs, grasses, mushrooms, bark from trees, and as I walked around I had to fight all kinds of animals. There were all sizes of small creatures that came at me.

After I took the time and got all of my things put away, I went back to the Garden and found Christophe hanging around.

"You've earned a reward for your work."

"Where did you go?"

"I can't tell you where I went. I have a place that no one knows about. When the heat comes down, I have a place to go to, and I need that protection. It gives me an alibi if I'm not around."

"I get you, so when you give me a job, you run to your place, so you won't be questioned."

"You're smart, here's $300.00 gold reward and you're promoted to Bandit."

"Thanks."

There's another fence Dar Jee who lives in Leyawiin. And you can go see S'krivva in Bravil he will give you work also.

I figured what the hell, I needed to get out and meet people, and this was the best way to do it. I ran all the way to Bravil's North gate and then looked for S'krivva's home. I went from door to door looking for her home. When I found her home, I checked the door to see if it was locked and it wasn't so I let myself in. S'krivva was on elderly Khajiit woman and she sat knitting in a rocking-chair.

CHAPTER 3

AHDARJI'S RING

"Mama," I addressed her, "Would you have an assignment for this young bandit?"

"There is a lonely old widow by the name of Ahdarji, her late husband was a fence for the Thieves Guild and she lost a beloved ring to a street scavenger and is offering a reward for its safe return."

"I supposed that you would like me to find this ring for her"

"Yes, she is an old friend of mine, I have known her for a long time and she is a very dear friend."

"I will see if I can find her ring for her, since she is your friend."

"Thank you. Your efforts won't go unnoticed."

"Well, thanks for the vote of confidence"

I tossed her a $20.00 gold coin and left.

I walked around Bravil until I found just the street beggar I needed.

I went into my purse and pulled out a gold coin worth $20.00 and handed it to him.

"What is your name kind sir?" I asked him.

He replied, "Dee the Scalawag".

"I need to find Ahdarji and I was wondering if you could help me."

"You will need to go to the West side of town; she will be eating lunch at the Five Claws Lodge from noon until 2:00 pm."

"Do you know where I can find her after that?"

I have been told that she eats dinner at the Three Sisters Lodge and she stays there until around midnight." "Thanks for your help."

"That is the best that I can do for you."

"You have been plenty of help."

While I was waiting for the time to find Ahdarji, I broke into Alval Uvani's and Rosentia Gallenius' house and then I met with Dar Jee and sold everything for $200.00 gold.

I finally found Ahdarji.

"I have been told that you need help with a ring, ma'am. Is there anything that this poor thief can do to help you?"

"Another thief", she said to me with a hint of disgust in her voice.

"Ma'am, I can assure you that I am unlike any thief that you have ever met or read about, I want to help you; it just so happens that until I can boost my skills I am working for the Thieves Guild."

"Well," she softened up a little, "I do want the thief who stole my ring dead."

"I'm not a killer ma'am just a thief." I told her as confidently as I could.

"If you can," she said to me, "The thief has to at least suffer."

"All I can give you right now; is a name, Amusei."

She was the young woman who was with me in the Garden when I was trying to get into the Thieves Guild initially.

I went back to Dee the Scalawag

"Hey Dee," I said to him as I tossed him another $20.00 gold coin.

"I was wondering if you could help me again."

"I will surely try my young friend."

"I am trying to help Ahdarji and return a stolen ring to her."

"Well, I do know that her ring was stolen. She made a big to do about it the other day."

"Do you know who stole it?"

"No, I don't but I do know that Amusei was the one who was arrested and thrown in jail, pinched you might say. I heard that she was also trying to blackmail Leyawiin's Countess."

The guard also threw in the wisdom that they could be bribed to allow a visitor to see a prisoner. So I made my way to the castle dungeon where I was refused admittance to see Amusei before I could even ask. I quickly tendered a $20 bribe. Then I offered Amusei a lockpick. She told me about the ring that she tried to steal and where I could find it. So I thought that I would go visit Ahdarji and ask more about the ring. She told me that her attachment to the ring was more than sentimental. She also told me that the ring allowed the wearer to read the Count's private messages. Then she said that she would gladly pay me double for its return. The countess rarely leaves the castle; and I was wished good luck in getting it back.

Going back to the mage's guild I asked if I could buy a fortify agility spell and have it combined with a soul trap; I was told that it would cost me $500 gold. I walked out to the edge of town and cast the spell on myself and raised my agility to 2050 just like my strength.

Checking with Dee the Scalawag he mentioned that there was a secret hidden torture chamber used for interrogation of Argonian immigrants from Black Marsh plus a secret entrance into the Countess's bed chamber and she puts her rings in a jewelry box at night.

The secret passage links the cellar to the royal quarters. I could use the door in the castle lobby's southwest corner to reach the cellar. In the storage room at the end of the hall I threw the switch in the barrel against the west wall to open the secret door nearby and followed the hall beyond to the torture chamber then continued to the royal quarters.

I had to use basic caution as I had nothing but locks to deal with along the way. The only serious obstacle was the jewelry box. It had a tough lock but I did manage to get it open.

I then grabbed the ring and a document "Divining the Elder Scrolls" from the jewelry box and got out of there, going back the way that I came and made my way first to Ahdarji and then to S'krivva for their separate rewards and a promotion to "Prowler"

CHAPTER 4

HIERONYMUS LEX AND I

Then I went to Ungolim's house in Bravil to loot it. I looted the whole place. I went back to Dar Jee and sold him a good bit of what I stole and there was still some left over to go to other fences.

Hieronymus Lex was the Imperial Watch Captain and he had no tolerance for the Thieves Guild and put out a bounty on the Gray Fox. Guards from all over the city were patrolling the Waterfront District when I got there. The guards put a curfew in effect. Christophe was under house arrest and Methredhel was handling all Thieves Guild business for the time being, and she sent word that she wanted to see me.

She told me that five guild operatives were going to stage simultaneous burglaries around the city; I was to steal Hrormir's staff from the Arch-Mage's room at the Arcane University and leave a note from Gray Fox.

It was easy. I went to the top-most room in the central Arch-Mage's tower while Hannibal Traven was in the council of mages. I took the staff from the table and activated it and left the note. I collected a document fragment "The Song of Hrormir" and helped myself to as much as I could carry while I was there.

I went back to Methredhel,

As I handed her the staff, "Here is the staff that you wanted me to get for you."

"Thank you dear, you are such a wonderful thief. I don't think that anyone else in this can compete with your skills. It seems to come so natural to you. You truly are a gifted thief."

"Thank you, Methredhel."

"I have another job for you if you want it."

"Sure, what is it that you want me to do?"

"I need for you to spy on Hieronymus Lex and learn as much as you can about his doings."

"Sure thing, I'll report back to you in a few days."

"You do that and good luck."

I went back to my place first and dropped off everything that I didn't need and took a nap. I woke up a few hours later and was offered another chance to level up.

Even the best thieves and burglars can get up in a pinch sometimes. It happened to me one night. It was Hieronymus' home and I was taking my time going through his things when I heard the tumblers in his lock begin to move.

I looked around, where do I go? I can't get out of here, there is only one door, and he is at it. I was on my way to becoming the world's best thief but I had a long way to go, and if I wound up in the slammer now, that would put an early end to my career.

I wasn't frightened or scared. I was nervous and a little bit anxious. I had seconds before the door opened and there I would be standing in the middle of Lex's house. Then I remembered, I had purchased a ring a few days ago, that gave the wearer a cloak of invisibility. I reached into my pocket and there it was, just by pure chance it was in my pocket and I slipped it on my finger and the spell took effect just as the door swung open.

I was purely invisible to the naked eye. I watched as Lex went about his business and I sat in a corner by the door. And I waited for him to go to sleep. Once he was asleep, I crept out into the darkness.

In the morning, I then went back to the Waterfront District and started following Lex and while I was doing so, a Dremora appeared to the north walked up to him and offered him a note.

Lex read the note and got a weird look on his face then dropped the note letting it skitter away in the breeze. I retrieved the note and read it. The note was from Raminus Polus of the Mages guild and it wasn't so much an order as a threat. But the threat worked. Lex called off his dogs.

CHAPTER 5

"LOST HISTORIES OF TAMRIEL"

Returning to Methredhel, I gave her the note and she told me that she had one last job for me. I was to return the staff but in the home of Ontus Vanin.

My reward was $800 gold and a promotion to Cat Burglar and a new fence. His name was Luciana Galena in Bravil and I had $600 gold to spare. S'krivva was at the Lonely Suitor lodge from noon to 2 AM. S'krivva had asked me to go to Skingrad to retrieve a book called the "Lost Histories of Tamriel" for the Gray Fox. I ran to Skingrad and found a beggar named Foul Fagus and bribed him with $20 gold. He told me that I should get a job at the jail in order to see a prisoner named Theranis.

So I went to the Castle and asked an Imperial about working in the castle. I was referred to Shum gro-Yarug who hired me as "slop drudge" who brought food to the prisoners. Shum gave me a description of tasks and prohibitions, and then I could go to work. I looked for the dungeon door up the stairs to my left in the castle courtyard. I identified myself to the jailer and he admitted me to the cellblock. I looked all over the place for Theranis but he wasn't there so I told a lone inmate named Larthjar the Laggard that I was there to rescue him. He told me that the "pale lady" had taken Theranis from the jail three times and the last time he didn't come back.

He told me to follow the blood on the floor. It led up to a blank wall at the hall's end. I searched for a lever and found an odd looking candle, pulled it and a secret door opened. I entered what looked like an old wine cellar. I immediately went into sneak mode. Then I followed the other hall which ended in another wall. I pulled the handle to the left and it opened another secret door. I was in what looked like the butler's quarters. The bloodstains continued into the cask room.

Once there, I tried to activate the rightmost of the three scones to open the front of the central cask. Moving cautiously down the passage I came upon the "pale lady" and the flimsy Vampire. I fought them both and made quick work of it.

I found Theranis' dead body and searched it and found a note. It said, "Amusei's grateful for your rescue and says that she'll join the guild. She has a message for the guild from Theranis which he'll pass along if you get him out.

Returning the way that I came, I left the castle, crossed the bridge and I headed down the path toward Skingrad. Halfway down the hill, I got a mental message which told me to "look under the bush near the well behind Nerastarel's house." The message was right. The "Lost Histories of Tamriel" was near the well behind the house between a bush and a rock. I took a look at it then put it away. I then returned to S'krivva and he gave me $400 gold.

My next job was to eliminate Lex. As it so happens Anvil's countess was looking for a new guard captain. The commander of the Imperial Watch had sent her a list of candidates. The list did not carry a strong recommendation for Lex; who through his own heavy hand and the guild's own concerted efforts appeared as something of a screw-up. This letter has arrived in Anvil and currently resided in the desk of Dairihill, Countess Umbranox's steward.

S'krivva said to me, "The Gray Fox wants you to steal the list and find a forger who can create a new one with Flieronymus Lex's name at the top of the list."

"I've been around, and I know a lot of people since I have been here, but I have yet to meet a forger."

"Going to the Anvil Mage's Guild Methredhel sent us to, "The Stranger" who lived near Mages guild he would be the best bet."

I asked around for the "Stranger" and it took several people several gold coins to get me going in the right direction.

"Sir," I said as I approached him, "I was sent to you by The Gray Fox and he would like for you to do a job for him."

"Do you have any proof that you are sent by the Gray Fox?"

"No sir, I do not."

"Well, man, it is going to cost you extra, let this be a lesson to ya, when the Gray Fox sends you on a job, you best take some proof that he be the one who sent ye."

"Yes sir."

"Just so you know, I don't work for just anybody, so anyone else be sending you around; you make sure that they are on the up and up."

"I hear you."

"We'll hear this too, you are going to have to spend, $1500 today. Are you prepared to spend that for not thinking about what the Fox wants from you?"

"Sir, yes I am," I said as I handed him the document.

"Here is the $1500 and the Fox wants you to put Hieronymus Lex's name at the top of the list."

"Well, son, I am going to need 24 hours minimum to do this job, so skedaddle and see me tomorrow."

"I'll see you tomorrow then." And I walked away.

I took a break, went home fixed something to eat and went to sleep. Waking up I was able to increase my attributes.

CHAPTER 6

SAVILLA'S STONE

I returned to the man known as 'The Stranger" picked up the new document and went back to the steward's office and replaced the document.

I went back to S'krivva and I was given $600 gold and a promotion to 'Shadowfoot' and the name of a new fence.

I heard later that afternoon that Hieronymus Lex was promoted to Captain of Countess Umbranox's bodyguard.

Hanging around Bravil scoping out Ungolim's house waiting for the prime opportunity to loot it, Methredhel came up to me and told me that the Gray Fox had a job for me and he wanted me to meet him at Helvius Cecia's house in Bruma, so I went to the market and unloaded everything I had for $500 gold and gave the shopkeeper $100 of it back to increase his disposition towards me and knowing that as I was able to increase my mercantile skills, it would pay off later.

When I got to Cecia's house he was waiting outside for me. He told me the Gray Fox was inside. I went inside. The Fox was sitting next to the fireplace with a Gray Cowl hiding his face like a veil.

"Greetings Sir," I addressed him.

"I need you to go on a retrieval mission for me."

"I want a great crystal called Savilla's Stone from the Temple of Ancestor Moths; it is an extensive and well-guarded monastery in the mountains of Northeast Cyrodiil."

"After getting the stone meet me here again."

As usual, I found a beggar and offered him $20.00 gold to fill me in on the information that I needed and I was given more than what I needed.

Finding the stone was easy, and getting it out was even easier. I climbed to the top of the tower and tied a rope to the latch on top and climbed down to the stone. I snatched up the stone and climbed back out. I returned to Bruma and the Gray Fox.

CHAPTER 7

ARROW OF EXTRICTION

He told me to stay put for a while and I took advantage of the time to loot Lyra Rosenita's house and also looted Honmund's house and Baelin's house as well. I went to Laciana Galena and sold everything to him for $1,000 gold.

I needed some sleep so I went to the inn grabbed a room and caught a few hours' sleep.

Then came a knock at my door and it was Amusei.

"You are to meet the Fox at Malintus Ancrus' house in Chorrol."

My next job was to steal the Arrow of Extriction from Bravil Court wizard Fathis Aren. Accepting the mission I was once again on my way to the old city.

I found a beggar who could tell me about Aren and he told me about a ruined tower outside of town where he stored his choicest treasures and there was a tunnel linking his castle to the tower.

1 figured that the castle was the place to start.

I went to the north wing picked the lock on the middle door on the balcony above the castle lobby. I put myself in sneak and opened the door. There were two guards flanking the door but didn't even notice me.

1 took a left and found another door, picked the lock and was in Aren's chambers. I picked two locks, found more locks and picked and picked without any clue as to the secret door. Finally, opposite the door on the right hand column just beyond was another locked door that led to the Wizard's Grotto.

At the first junction there was a creature to sneak past and a door to pick.

I took the left two ramps curving down to a broad watery channel and continued south until I saw the floor fall away ahead of me. I had to look for an exit that was initially hidden by overhanging rocks.

Once past the point everything was obvious if I wasn't in sneak, I would have to face more conjurers and a Daedra as well.

In the Wizard's lair which was a large room with stairs in the back right corner that led up to the tower entrance. I had to climb to the top of the stairs against the north wall. And then drop a level on the gap's far side.

I slipped past Aren into his Alchemy Lab, opened the chest in the right rear corner and swiped the tower key and the Arrow of Extrication.

Returning to the Fox, I gave him the arrow, he gave me $500 gold and promoted me to Master-Thief, and he gave me the name and the location of the last of the five fences; who was Fathis Ules and he was based out of Elven Gardens.

I thought that I would hang out in Chorrol for a little while. After some time passed I decided to loot the Orum house in Cheydinhal and Rimalus Bruiant's house in Chorrol and the Nerastarel's house in Skingrad and fence as much as I could to Fathis and build a relationship with him.

CHAPTER 8

THE BOOTS OF SPRINGHEEL JAK

I thought it best to wait around to see if someone would approach me for a mission. I took a nap first so that I could level up.

After leveling up, Amusei showed up and told me that he had a request from Gray Fox and he wanted to meet me at Ganredhep's house in Cheydinhal.

He began by telling me who Springheel Jak was and that when he died he had been buried with his boots on, and that these boots possessed magic in them and I was to find the grave and recover the boots.

My usual fare was to find a beggar in the area and trade in the commodity known as information, and I had to pay one $20.00 gold piece before I learned that Jak's only living descendant was the Earl of Imbel and that he lived in Talos Plaza, which was in Imperial City.

I stopped by the Mage's Guild and bought a daylight spell that cost me $500 gold.

I found my way to Talos Plaza and the Earl's home and picked the lock and let myself in. Axius was there and he told me that the Earl would be home shortly.

I waited and then the door burst open and there stood Jak and he said to me, "Now you will die." I chopped his head off and cast the daylight spell and his body burst into flames.

I took his boots from him and I put them on, and they boosted my Acrobatics by 50 points raising my Acrobatics to 100, I returned to Gray Fox, and he gave me $500 gold, and he told me that I could keep the boots.

Traveling to the Waterfront I ran into Amusei who invited me to meet with the Gray Fox one last time at Otherlo's house in the Northeast Corner in the Imperial City's Elven Gardens.

CHAPTER 9

THE ELDER SCROLL

He wanted me to steal an Elder Scroll from the Imperial Palace, something that no one had ever accomplished and probably only ever considered. Considering the amount of security there is in the palace.

The Gray Fox said that he needed the scroll for himself. It would take a string of difficult tasks for me to accomplish this. The Elder Scrolls were kept behind a door that couldn't be opened.

Savilla's stone which I had liberated from the Temple of the Ancestor Moths revealed an old forgotten way around the door once called the "Old Way". The entrance to the "Old Way" is sealed. To unseal it, I had to find the "Glass of Time" in the palace cellars and activate it.

He told me that I would also need the boots that I had just retrieved and the Arrow of Extrication.

What I needed to do is buy some more spells from the mages guild before I left. I chose 'Open Hard Lock', 'Summon Scamp', and 'Summon Ghost'.

CHAPTER 10

JOINING THE FIGHTER'S GUILD

I thought that I should go find a way to increase some of other skills, and I joined the "Fighter's Guild".

My first quest was called the "Rat Problem".

I then went to Arvena Thelas' house and fought a mountain lion in her cellar.

"There is a hunter who lives down the street from me whose name is Penarus Inventius, he might be able to help you."

I went to Penarus's house to talk to him.

"Penarus, I need your help. There is a lady named Arvena down the street from you and she is being plagued by mountain lions, and I want to help her."

"I can take you to a spot where lions will always appear and we'll see what happens."

So I walked with him to the area and two lions attacked when we approached and Penarus showed his skill by quickly dispatching one.

Afterwards, I went back to Arvena.

Penarus and I went to a wooded area just outside of town, and killed two lions just an hour ago. You should be safe for now."

"I don't think so. I forgot to mention to you earlier that there is woman named Quill-Weave who has been sneaking around at night behind my house. Maybe she has something to do with all of this."

Just before dark I went out in the back of Arvena's house and hid in the bushes and shortly before 8PM an Argonian woman showed up, I jumped out of the bushes and confronted her.

"I didn't want hurt anyone and you sure put a fright into me."

"What are you doing out here this late at night and alone and creeping around like you are up to no good?"

"I was leaving meat outside so that I could lure lions into Arvena's basement to eat her rats. I just wanted to help her with her problem. I didn't want to make it worse."

"Well you sure did make it worse."

"I know, I know."

"I want you to stop leaving meat outside, the rats are not a pest for Arvena, and they are her pets. You have been killing animals that she loves and cares for as if they were her family."

"I am so sorry, I just didn't know."

"Well now you do, and I will expect you to stop."

"Please don't tell anyone and I will raise your skill in acrobatics to a level 40."

"Well, I think that I can manage that."

I went back to Arvena.

"Arvena, Quill-Weave is just going for nightly walks"

"It sure seems quite sneaky."

"She just likes going for walks at night. She thinks about her days and what she wants for tomorrow and the peace and quiet of the moonlit sky sets her at ease."

"I hope that she is able to make her life better then."

"You bet, everyone deserves a good life"

I went back to Quill-Weave and she helped me boost my skill level to 40 for free. This gave me 120 points to add to my attributes.

CHAPTER 11

THE NIGHT I ROBBED NORBET LELLES

I went back to Azzan at the Guild and asked for a promotion and another job. The promotion was given and the job was to help a shopkeeper who was having a problem with burglars. It just happened that it was Norbert Lelies store in Anvil. The door was left open, I looted the store myself and waited for the bandits to arrive, when they did, I defeated them, and I left their bodies where they lay. And I went to my shack and unloaded everything that I was carrying except the essentials, and returned to loot the bandit's bodies and waited around for Norbert to come back and wondered if he would notice that all of his stuff was missing. Apparently he didn't, I convinced Norbert to buy from me all the swag from the bandits and even gave him a discount, and less than what he wanted to give me for it.

Then I went back to my shack and picked up everything that I dropped off and repaired my weapons and armor and other loot before heading off to the fence Ongar.

Ongar took everything that I had and we haggled for the best price I could get from him, which came to around $3,000 gold.

I then returned to the Fox and told him that I felt that I was ready for the task.

CHAPTER 12

THE THEFT OF THE ELDER SCROLL

I went into the Elder Council Chambers and hung a left and following the ring corridor to a locked door that led to a crypt. There were two guards; sneak mode was the only way to get past them.

Activating the Glass told me that I had to begin in the Arboretum.

I was at the door that led to the east into the Arena district. A gate led down to the South East tunnel just north of the path. I used it.

In the sewer, I followed the passage north and east to a gate with a lock. I picked it.

In the room beyond there was a wheel in the west wall to open a door in the east.

Beyond the door, I dropped into a trench and headed north.

I moved cautiously up to an opening that was called "Beneath the Bloodworks". I assumed that it meant that I was below the Arena and in the sewers.

I opened the door to the east and descended the stairs into a room with gates to the east and the south.

Both passages were blocked and there was a wolf that I had to kill, and there were stairs to climb to a room with a corridor to another gate.

Inside, I turned a wheel in the room and it opened a gate to the north, I dropped off the bridge and headed east through a mechanical gate.

Across the trench room with a closed north exit to a gated room with another wheel in the north wall.

Turning the wheel to open the north exit from the trench room I used the exit and took a western passage to a locked gate, it opened with the key I received from the Gray Fox.

In the middle of the room a manhole lead to the Palace Sewers. Activating the cover I descended looking for the entrance to the Old Way.

I opened the gate, descended the stairs and headed north through a second gate to a pair of cisterns and crossed another trench.

On the far side of the trench just right of the bridge in an area where the sewer wall had collapsed revealed a "strange door" to the Old Way.

The Old Way was a tomb. With numerous undead from Skeletons to Wraiths, roaming the hallways which were also booby-trapped with swinging mace traps and heavily locked doors.

I gradually made my way south to the entrance to the Lost Catacombs.

Getting out was a lot more tricky than getting in.

Not taking anything for granted, I explored every nook and cranny looking for the entrance to the Lost Catacombs.

The Entrance was artfully concealed.

In the Southwest corner was a well, looking south from the well, and a section of sandy sub-structure where loose soil had been collecting from the walls.

The last niche on the left was not a niche at all but a ramp leading down to the final door.

Part palace crawlspace, part cave, and part Ayleid ruin the area was full of dead bodies and rats.

I saw the exit off in the distance.

Without Jak's boots there would not have been any way to open the door. Using the ruined staircase jumping up to the balcony where the switches are located, I was able to open the Iron Gate to the Hall of Epochs.

These same switches also activated two Dark Welkynd Stones that flanked the exit.

They fired chain lightning at me in strength that was equal to my own.

The only strategy was to run for the corners while they regenerated.

I got an idea that somehow the Arrow of Extrication was needed for this job.

I unlocked the side gate in the east wall of the upper level. This led to a balcony. There was a block at the balcony's south end that could be moved and it opened a secret door in the room below leading to a large chamber.

In the southwest corner were descending stairs, I went all the way to the bottom. Where I found a niche that contained the Elder Scroll.

At the east end of the room behind an altar was another block that could be pushed and doing so revealed nothing.

Retracing my steps, I encountered Zombies.

When I got to the big room with the statue the stone walls at the north end were gone.

These walls were blocking access to a bridge that was not noticeable when I walked underneath it before.

In the center of the bridge was a pressure plate, standing on the plate, the statue at the far end of the room did a 180 degree turn and a hatch opened in its belly exposing what looked like a keyhole.

I took aim with the Arrow of Extrication and hit my target and the statue rose into the air revealing a flight of stairs down into the fireplace of the Palace Guard Barracks.

I opened the door as quietly as possible, peering in most of the guards were asleep.

Bearing left down the hall I found a little ramp way that led to the Palace Library.

Returning to the Guild with the Elder Scroll I was given a cowl that carried three enchantments. 1) Boosting my Sneak skill by 25 points, 2) detect life spell, and 3) and a feather spell increasing encumbrance by 200 points.

I went back to the Mage's Guild for some more apprentice spells like: Fortify Speed, per 10, Personality, per 10, Willpower, per 100, Endurance per 100 and Intelligence per 100 coupled with Soul Trap to increase my overall abilities. I also acquired Ghost which cost me $3000 gold.

CHAPTER 13

THE SIREN'S

I thought that it was time that I check out The Siren's Deception and take the women for a ride next.

I had heard through the rumor mill that Faustina Cartia has been luring men to her home and robbing them.

I made my way to the hilltop farmhouse and waited until 11PM to enter and confront Faustina, she drew and knife to attack me. Two women came out of nowhere to join her in the attack.

I summoned four ghosts to help me defend myself. It only took a few minutes to vanquish these women.

I looted their dead bodies, cleaned out the farmhouse and sold all of the items to a nearby merchant and got $300 gold.

The dagger Witsplinter was able to net me $2,000 gold pieces.

I went back to Azzan and he sent me over to Burz gro-Khash at the Cheydinhal branch of the guild.

Burz wanted me to deliver a bow, a hammer, and a sword to a trio of unarmed fighters Guild members in the Desolate mine.

After I got to the mine Rienna took the bow from me, a High Elf took the sword and the Ore took the hammer from me.

I decided to stay and help them clean out the mine.

1 went back to Burz and he promoted me to Journeyman.

Burz then sent me to the Chorrol chapter of the guild to talk to Vilena Donton.

1 was then sent to see Modryn Oreyn in the lower level of the guild. He told me of a new guild member named Maglir who had defaulted on a contract out in Skingrad; he wanted me to find out why.

I found Maglir at the West Weald Inn and he told me that the job was too dangerous and that if I wanted it I could have it.

He told me that I had to go into Fallen Rock Cave and retrieve Brenus Astis' journal without letting any boulders crush me.

Well, it seemed a simple enough job; go join the Mage's Guild and get them to give me a few protection spells.

I was sent to Marie Palielle and Skingrad's Great chapel of Julianos.

She was on the upper floor of the Chapel, I asked her for Heal Minor Wounds and Minor Respite and they cost me $100 gold pieces each.

Going back to Maglir to get the location of the cave, I got the directions and found the cave.

I crept in the cave walking cautiously so as not to disturb anything or cause any boulders to come loose, I found the journal and found my way back out in no time at all.

I headed back to Anvil with the journal and gave it to Oreyn.

He told me about a problem in Leyawiin and told me to talk to three guild members at the Five Claw lodge.

I found out that three men were angry over being displaced by the Blackwood Company.

There was a woman named Margarte outside of town who did not trust either the Fighter's Guild or the Blackwood Company.

I stopped by the All Things Alchemy store and bought five portions of ectoplasm. She told me that she would consider her position if I acquired for her five portions of Ectoplasm and I immediately gave her the ones I had and she told me that she would stand with the Fighter's Guild. She also told me that she would give me $500 gold pieces for each group of 5 Ogre's teeth and Minotaur horns.

Went I got back to Oreyn he promoted me to Swordsman, and sent me back to Azzan. This quest also brought to my mind that I needed to work on my alchemical skills.

CHAPTER 14

SOME RECENT CRIMES

Azzan told me about some recent thefts in the area and he wanted me to ask around.

Starting with talking to Guild members, I found out that member Newheim the Portly was a victim of a crime. I had to go all the way to the Waterfront District to be able to talk to him.

He told me that the thieves were "Wood Elves" and that they had stolen an heirloom that had been in the Portlies for three generations. It was a flagon that keeps ale 'cold and sweet'.

He believed that the bandits could be found in the Hrota Cave north of Anvil.

The cave was on the Southeast face of the great dark rock.

I summoned several ghosts to help me if I needed them. My marksmanship skills had improved over the past few weeks and I knew that it would come in handy in the cave. When I fired the first shot the ghosts that I had summoned quickly took off and dispatched the elves.

I went in and found the heirloom and returned it to Newheim.

Azzan bumped me up to protector and sent me back to Burz gro-Khash.

Burz asked me to go to Biene Ameilion in the small settlement of Water's Edge far down on the Lower Niben's west side.

Biene was in the northernmost of the houses.

Ameilion's father was a gambler; he had not very much luck and fallen into deep debt. Her father had vanished and the reason was not clear, she needed me to sell her grandfather's enchanted sword and cuirass to pay off her father's debt. She told me that her grandfather's burial site was to the southeast on the Eastern shore of the Lower Niben and consists of two sections. I told her that I would be right back. What I did was, I went to Skingrad to "All Things Alchemy" and bought five Minotaur horns and five Ogre's teeth for $100 gold and took them to Margaret who gave $500 gold for each set make the total $1000 gold. I took the $1000 gold and gave it to Ameilion for the debt.

CHAPTER 15

BUYING MY FIRST HOUSE

I had heard that a young man named Velwyn Benirus was selling his family home for $5,000 gold pieces and I decided to buy it. I had heard that he frequents the Counts Arms from about noon until midnight; I met up with him there and gave him what he wanted for the deed.

I went to my little shack that I had first settled into and collected all of my belongings and was happy that I now had a place to call my own with a deed.

While I was heading back to my new house, I was jumped by a couple of bandits and had to fight them off.

After about another 3 miles, these giant rats came out of nowhere and tried to have me for lunch.

Going to my new home, it was a wreck of a house. I unloaded all of the items that I had been carrying and laid down for a nap, and no sooner than I had done so when I was awoken by several ghosts and I had to kill them. I collected their ectoplasm.

When the fight was over, I heard a crash downstairs, when I went into the parlor I had found a vase that had fallen exposing a skeletal hand and a page from a diary. I put the hand in my pack and read the page.

There was a reference to a page that there was a door in the home that only a Benirus could open,

I looked for the diary that the page had fallen out of and found it on a shelf; in it, it revealed that Velwyn's grandfather was a necromancer and a grave robber.

I went to find Velwyn and found him at the King and Queen tavern in the Elven Garden district. He followed me back to his former home and did his magic and disappeared.

In the room was an altar and I placed the hand on the altar and a figure appeared and began a chant. I laid into the ghastly figure and ended its existence.

In the cellar room, I found Lorgren's staff, The Tome of Unlife and 3 gems, 4 necklaces and a sack of gold next to the altar.

When I emerged from the cellar, the home had been transformed. The shutters and the paintings had been rehung. The walls were intact, and there was food on the table.

Going to the guild in Skingrad, I found Adrienne who had told me that she had lent some notes to Erthor and wanted me to get them back for her. He lived in Bleak Falls Cave. The cave being northwest of Skingrad. She taught me "Weak Fireball" before I left just in case I needed it.

Once inside his cave, I found it full of Zombies. I laid waste to many of them making my way to Erthor, and he told me that he would not return with me until I had cleared out all of the Zombies. So this I did.

Adrienne then sent me off to Leyawiin.

I was met outside the front door of the mage's guild by Agata and she told me of an amulet that was taken from her by the Arch Mage Dagail and she asked me to get it back for her.

Agata helped me with three new spells. "Summon Spider Daedra with Soul Trap", "Fire Storm 100 points", and "Heal Superior Wounds", this all cost me $2000 gold.

She told me that the amulet was taken to for Blueblood southeast of Leyawiin.

When I got to the cave, I went into sneak and I summoned a bunch of Spider Daedra to help with the target. It was over in seconds.

I returned the amulet to Agata and took a nap, and leveling up.

The next morning Agata told me that I had to go to Chorrol.

CHAPTER 16

THE DAY THAT I SPENT AT CHORROL

On the way, I stopped at the Cloud Top Mountains and the Nonwyll Cavern. A cave full of Trolls, Ogres, a Minotaur and this meant money from Margarte.

Before creeping into the cave I summoned so many Spider Daedra and Ghosts there was no room to stand. I crept into the cave as easy and as lightly as I could. Inching my way along, I made it all the way to the innermost part of the cave before unleashing everything I could on the Minotaur and the Spiders and the Ghosts went to work on the Trolls and Ogre's and when it was all over with there were: two Minotaur horns, several portions of ectoplasm, Ogre teeth, Daedra venom, and Daedra silk for me to collect and sell.

There was a dead body and the broken shield of Galtus Previa and I returned it to Oreyn who rewarded me with a Magic Blade.

Oreyn told me that Maglir was not doing the jobs he was given by mage Aryarie. I reported to the mage and he told me that Maglir had joined the Blackwood Company and that he wanted me to get 10 portions of Imp Gull from the Robber's Glen Cave and return them to him.

Aryarie gave me a ring of shielding.

Oreyn promoted me to the rank of defender. He also told me that he wanted to expose the Blackwood Company as the imposters they were. So I told him that I would save him the trouble and he told me that Azani had a ring that he wanted.

Azani left behind a Daedra Claymore and the ring which I gave to Oreyn and he promoted me to Warden and sent me off to Azzan again.

Azzan told me about the scholar Elante of Alinor who was researching Daedra worship. She needed an escort to Brittlerock Cave near the Fort Sutch and protection while she worked.

After clearing out the caves for her she decided to stay so I went back to Azzan.

He told me that I had to return to Burz gro-Khash, he wanted me to go to Bloodmayne cave, kill the fugitives and save the hostages.

After I did as he asked gro-Khash gave me advancement to Guardian and back to Oreyn.

CHAPTER 17

THE TRIAL OF THE FORSAKEN MINE

Oreyn sent me off to investigate the Trolls of Forsaken Mine. He told me that he had already sent a team and had not heard back from them.

Before going into the mine I summoned some spider's to help me with the trolls. I found the three guild members dead. Donton's body had a journal with him. I looted everything.

I went back to Oreyn and he told me to wait a few days and go back to Azzan.

I went home and caught some sleep and a level up.

After meeting up with Azzan he told me that Oreyn had been kicked out of the guild and that I had been demoted to defender.

I was sent to recover a stone that was stolen from a Church in Bruma.

I went to Bruma and met up with Cirror who told me that a Ward against Evil was taken.

Some men were seen heading east the night it was taken.

I followed the road and met up with a Khajiit named K'Sharra who told me that some humans had jumped him and taken his cart.

Continuing on the road, I found the stone and ran back to Azzan who told me about another job; this time rescuing a Noble's daughter.

Running off to Cheydinhal the Lord told me that some Ogre's ran off with his daughter and he told me to go east. I quickly found them and killed them with the Claymore.

The Lord of the Manor gave me Rugdumph's Sword after I returned his daughter.

Next I was sent to Drarana Thelis in Harlun's Watch. She wanted me to check out some weird lights in and around the area of Swampy Cave. When I got to the area I summoned a bunch of Spiders again and had them help me dispatch the Will-O-the-Wisps.

When it was over, I collected the dust and returned to Burz who promoted me to Champion.

I was then back to Chorrol to speak with Oreyn, he wanted me to kidnap Ajum Kajin a Blackwood Leader at the company's new base in Glademist Cave.

After disposing of several of the Blackwood guards, Kajin agreed to follow me back to Oreyn, who told me to take a walk.

The ship Serpent's Wake was waiting for me. I summoned several ghosts to keep me company while I was on the ship. Sure enough a spectral sailor passed me on the ship's deck.

CHAPTER 18

THE SERPENT'S WAKE

Walking around I found locks to pick and chests to open. I found a key on the Captain's body, found a 100 pieces of gold, magic jewelry, a jade necklace. I shot at a guard who was at his post and the ghosts got rid of him, and I found a chest in the room with a crystal in it.

I knocked off everyone on the ship and looted all of the crates and chests before returning to Oreyn.

Oreyn told me that I needed to go to the Blackwood Company and join them and spy on them.

I found the number two man Jeetum-Zee and the Company Building in Leyawiin. He asked me some questions and then told me to follow him to the training hall.

He told me about getting rid of some goblins at the Hamlet on the Water's Edge. There were several other guild members there and we were sent to kill these goblins. There must have been at least a dozen.

I awoke to find myself looking at the face of Modryn Oreyn who told me that guild member brothers found me unconscious on the streets of Leyawiin and I told him about the goblins at Water's Edge.

We went back to Water's edge and I found Biene Ameilion, Jolie,

Edward Retiene and Marie Alouette all dead.

I went back to the Company Building summoned so many spiders there was no way that anyone at Blackwood would make it out alive.

Ja'fazir was first, and Jeetum-Zee and Ri'Aakar two Argonian mages and Hist Thee, and even Maglir.

After I made it back to Oreyn's house he gave me the Helm of Oreyn Bear Claw, then he sent me to the Guild Master Vilena Donton. She promoted me to Guild Master and named Oreyn as Second in Command.

After this, I was told that Janus Hassildor's requested my presence in Skingrad.

On the way I stopped off at a Mage's Guild and bought: Fire, Frost, Damage Magicka, and Fortify Magicka spells for $200 gold.

I ran to Cheydinhal and then to Vahtacen.

The Northbound Passage took me through the caves to the underground ruins.

Skaleel was waiting at her camp in the first large room. The problem was that researchers had found a pillar at the bottom of the explored ruins. The column responded to magic. I was lucky in that I just so happened to have picked up the spells that I needed on my way there.

I was gifted with an Ancient Elven Helm. I took this back to the Mage's Guild and I was promoted to Conjurer with a snazzy new robe. They took my helm from me for study.

While I was in Chorrol, a messenger arrived with news of Necromancer's Massing under the Necromancer's Moon. There was a cave in the mountains nearby known as the Dark Fisher, Polus asked me to go there to see what I could find.

When I got there I found a Worm Anchorite trading regular Soul Gems for Black ones. I went back to Polus and he promoted me to Magician. Then he sent me to Arch-Mage Traven. There I talked to Traven who sent me to the Ayleid Ruin's Nenyond Twyll and to bring Mucianus Allias back to the guild for questioning.

Once at the Nenyond Twyll ruins I quickly located Mucianus Allias. Halfway through the ruins I ran into Fithragaer and he told me that the Necromancers were waiting for the battlemages. With this advance warning, I summoned 20 Spider Daedra's and 10 Ghosts, and told Mucianus Allias to stay behind me, and we moved into the area where they were waiting to make the ambush and fired an arrow into one of the undead, then my minions killed everyone in sight.

When the battle was over, I strolled through the ruins with Mucianus Allias looting bodies. Afterwards, Mucianus Allias and I returned to Traven where I was promoted to Warlock.

After this I went to Bruma and stole from Lyra Rosenita's and Honmund and Beanlin's houses and fenced all of the looted and stolen property.

After I rested again, the dreams began to speak to me of Crowhaven ruins which sat on a hilltop and the only clue I had to go on was Malog. So I started asking around. I went to every place I had ever been and talked to anyone I had ever met and was finally told to go to the Arena when I was in Imperial City.

I was told to talk to the Gray Prince.

I told him of the dream of the hilltop ruins and Malog.

He told me that his full name is Agronak gro-Malog and that he is a Lord's son who has being denied his rightful position of being an heir and all that comes with it. He was a half-Orc and that he is the illegitimate child of Lord Lovidicus. His mother was an Ore servant in Lord Crowhaven's fortress in the western reaches of Cyrodiil, and they fled to the Imperial City when the Lord's wife threatened to kill them.

Before his mother died gro-Malog was given a key that would unlock the truth about his birthright at Crowhaven. He told me that if I helped him that he would grant me 3 points each to Athletics, Blade and Block skills.

I made for the ruins.

When I arrived, I summoned a dozen Spider Daedras and let them destroy any enemies in the area. I found a tower in the Northwest Corner. Down and down I went until I finally found a gate that could be unlocked by the key. I found a journal sitting on a table and put it in my bag.

CHAPTER 19

THE FIGHTS OF HONOR

Making it back to gro-Malog he felt that he had no reason to go on living after reading his father's journal but he kept his word. Then he told me to sign up for the bouts and that I should give him a warrior's death. So, I signed up. There were eight matches that I had to partake in. Each match was supposed to be tougher than the next, and for each match that I won, I would receive a monetary reward.

Match #1 was a female wood elf, a male Imperial, and an Argonian archer. From that match I was promoted to Brawler and given $150 gold.

Match #2 was a Nord, a Khajiit, and two wood elf sisters. From that match I was promoted to Bloodletter and given $200 gold.

Match #3 was a Redguard, Breton Lady. From that match I was promoted to Myrmidon and was given $250 gold.

Match #4 was a high elf, an Ogre, and from that match I was promoted to Warrior and was given $300 gold.

Match #5 was another Nord, two magic users and another Ogre. From that match I was promoted to Gladiator and was given $500 gold.

Match #6 was 3 Argonian prisoners, another Breton, and then from that match I was promoted to Hero and was given $600 gold.

Match #7 was a former Blade member and a orc. From that match I was promoted to Champion and was given $800 gold.

Match #8 was Grand Champion Ysabel Andronicus, beating him, from that match I was promoted to Grand Champion and was given $1000 gold.

I went home set up my goods and took a good night's sleep and was given another level up opportunity.

My next adventure in Cyrodiil was that of the Dark Brotherhood. I went to Riverview Mansion in Cheydinhal; I had to wait for the two servants Tanaso Arano and Tolish Girith to fall asleep. I went into their rooms killed them and looted their rooms.

Then I went to the Inn of 111 Omen and killed Rufio while he slept and looted his body and room, there was mostly junk so I didn't get too much for the stuff.

Then it was off to home again to sleep.

When I awoke, Lucien LaChance was in my room. LaChance looked at me and told me that I was already in the Dark Brotherhood.

He told me that Vicente Valtieri was a Vampire. I was to kill Captain Gaston Tussaud aboard his ship, the Marie Elena, which was docked in the Imperial City's Waterfront District. I was to kill the Captain. I decided to slip into a crate, so that when the supplies were brought aboard, I would be in a crate.

I waited until I felt that enough time has passed and then slipped out made my way to the middle deck then aft. I found a pair of pirates arguing about having a woman (Malvulis) aboard the ship. I waited until they were done talking and then when one of them started coming my way, while the other went further aft, I had to make my way back to the trap door.

I then was able to make my way to the Captain's quarters and then opened the door in sneak mode and putting a hurt on the old boy and took his key. I unlocked the chest on top of the dresser. Then I exited via the rear door onto the balcony and rear of the boat and dove into the murky waters of the Niben and swam back to shore.

I ran back to Valtieri and asked about my next mission.

He told me that I had to go to Bruma and help a resident have an accident. It was a specific task and if I pulled it off successfully there would be a bonus waiting for me.

Mr. Baelin was to have an accident; I was to sneak into his home and find a secret door that led to a space between the wall and the roof. I waited until he sat in his favorite chair underneath a Minotaur head and loosened the ties that held up the head and let the head fall, killing him.

I went down to the cellar and went out the back and returned to the Sanctuary where I was given the dagger Sufferthom with Damage Health and Damage Strength. I was also given $1,000 gold and was promoted to Slayer.

Valtieri told me that I had to go to the Imperial prison and kill Valen Dreth. He also told me that a prisoner had found a way to escape using the sewer system. He gave me a key and told me that if I avoided killing any guards there would be another bonus for me.

A trench room in the second section had a remote operation for a gate in the southeast. It also had a locked gate for the northeast. There was a door beyond the locked gate that led to the third and final section of the sewers.

There were still guards looking into the Emperor's assassination. I made my way quickly and quietly to the cells. And put an arrow through Valen Dreth and left.

Back at the sanctuary I received the Scales of Pitiless Justice as a bonus.

CHAPTER 20

FRANCOIS MOTIERRE

My next assignment was to "kill' Francois Motierre in Chorrol. He had gotten himself in trouble with loan sharks and an enforcer had been sent to serve justice.

Valtieri gave me a knife laced with the poison Langorwine on it, he told me that this simulates death and he gave me the antidote. When I got to Motierre's he told me that an Argonian had already been sent and his name was Hides-his-Heart. Sure enough moments later I heard Hides-his-Heart muttering something.

I quickly stabbed Motierre in front of Hides-his-Heart; he let out a crying sigh and slipped to the floor. I had to wait until midnight to find Motierre's body in the Chapel Crypt. I gave him the antidote, and then we made our way to The Gray Mare where Motierre booked passage out of Chorrol.

I went back to the Cheydinhal Sanctuary and Valtieri gave me an amulet called Cruelty's Heart. And then he told me to find Ocheeva for future quests. He also promoted me to Eliminator and gave me a key to the well beside an abandoned house. He told me that it would drop me into the northwest corner of the Sanctuary's main room.

My next mission was to kill a High Elf named Faelian, he lived in

Imperial City. Ocheeva told me the elves were a tight-knit community and that it would be difficult to find anyone willing to talk.

I went prepared to spend my gold.

I had to give an elf several hundred gold to get his disposition up to a point where he would open up to me.

He told me that Faelian lived at the Tiber Septim Hotel in Talos Plaza, that he was a rather "distasteful" fellow, and that he loved skooma and enjoyed visiting Lorkmir at his house on a regular basis.

I went to the hotel first and made an acquaintance with an elderly woman who was quite sad and raised her disposition and she began giving me compliments.

I went to the house of Lorkmir and snuck in killing him. Then I hid in the shadows waiting for Faelin to show up, when he closed the door, I shot the skooma smoking bastard.

I went back to Ocheeva informing him that the job was done. He gave me an enchanted steel bow as a bonus.

Ocheeva told me The Warlord Roderick lying deadly ill in the mercenary stronghold at Fort Sutch. I was to infiltrate the fort and replace the powerful medicine keeping him alive with a potent poison that he would supply.

There was a ruined tower near Fort Sutch and Ocheeva suspected that the flooded sewer ways were not guarded and suggested that I use them. I did so; I made my way through the fort to the room where Roderick lay. Out in the hall, I cast a number of spells over me to help hide me from his powerful magic and in sneak mode made my way around his bed and switched the medicine with the poison and backed out and ran back to Ocheeva. He gave me an enchanted shirt, "The Deceiver's Finery".

My next assignment was to kill everyone in a house where everyone was locked in expecting to play some game. The list of guests included: A young Dunmer lady, a Nord, Dovesi Dran, Nels the Naughty, the retired soldier Neville, the young nobleman Primo Antonius. Not necessarily a who's who but I did what I was asked. I cast spells of paranoia on them and began picking them off one at a time, ramping up the paranoia.

When it was all done I went back to Cheydinhal, the Night Mother gave me the Boots of Multiple Skills.

I went home got some sleep and leveled up.

CHAPTER 21

THE IMPERIAL LEGIONAIRE ADAMUS PHILLIDA

Now I was given an assassination assignment. I was to assassinate the Imperial Legion pest Adamus Phillida. I was given an arrow called the "Rose of Sithis" one shot one kill. Then I had to cut off his thumb and place it on the desk of his successor.

I had to follow this boring ass all day until he decided to go swimming and I cocked the arrow into my new bow and let it fly, I cut off his thumb, took his keys and armor. Then I took the thumb to the Imperial Headquarters.

Ocheeva then told me that I received sealed orders from Lucien LaChance.

I was to meet him at Fort Farragut.

What he told me sent me reeling. He told me that there was a traitor in our guild, I had to kill everyone in the guild, it was just going to be him and me and we were going to start over. He told me that it was an ancient rite called "Purification". I summoned Rufio's Angry Ghost for help in the matter and when it was over, I looted the place.

I went back to LaChance and told him that I had done what he asked.

He told me that the orders from now on would be done at dead-drops; the first would be in a hollow rock on Hero Hill. He promoted me to Silencer and gave me a Shadowmare, a black horse with glowing eyes.

I went home got some sleep, got some grub, and made some potions and worked on my alchemy skills.

Hero Hill was in the southeast, I had to go over some steep slopes. Inside I found orders to kill a Necromancer called Celedaen who was in the process of turning himself into a Lich. The orders hinted that he was way too powerful to confront directly. However, if I were to go into his cave, I might find some hint as to his weakness.

He lived in Leafrot Cave far to the south. I took the road to Lake Rumare and then headed south. His cave was just north of the Ayleid Ruin Morahame. Once in his cave, I cast spells of invisibility and chameleon and went into sneak mode, not far in, I found his journal. He titled his journal "The Path of Transcendence".

I read in his journal that he was using a magical hourglass to extend his life. I lifted it from him and summoned all kinds of creatures to help me rid the world of the monster.

I found my next set of instructions in a tree hidden in a sack south of Chorrol's north gate.

I was to kill off the entire Draconis family. Perennia the mother lived at Applewatch farm just west of

Bruma, posing as a delivery service she willingly gave me a list of addresses for her children.

I found my next orders on the gate by the well in Castle Skingrad's Courtyard. A Khajiit Nobleman

J'Ghasta has declined an offer of marriage and the girl's family wanted satisfaction.

CHAPTER 22

SHALEEZ THE ARGONIAN

I found my next set of orders on Red Wing Road. My next target was an Argonian hunter named Shaleez in the flooded mine just north of Bravil.

My next set of orders came from Fort Redman on the east bank of the lower Niben. I was to rid the world of Anvil Uvani a traveling merchant. He lived in southwest Leyawiin. I broke into his house and waited for him, and after killing him quickly, I looted his place and body, he had some pretty good stuff, so I was able to get some decent gold from the shopkeepers.

My next set of orders came from a hollow stump in a garden between Rindir's Staffs and Edgar's Discount Spells. My next stop was Gnoll Mountain east of Bruma. I was to kill Havilstein Hoar-Blood.

My next orders were in the Ayleid ruins of Nornal southeast of Cheydinhal. In Bravil, a Wood Elf Ungolim was in love with a married woman, the woman's husband asked the brotherhood to take care of the issue.

After killing Ungolim, Lucien LaChance told me that I was to go to the next dead drop and to get there before my orders arrived and confront the deliverer. Not long after I got there, a Wood Elf named

Enilroth showed up. I confronted him and he told me what he knew.

The lighthouse keeper was the one I had to see for the lighthouse cellar key. My orders were to assassinate a High Elf Whore named Arquen. Once inside the cellar I found a diary on the table. The traitor was a lunatic obsessed with obtaining revenge against LaChance and the Night Mother for the murder of his mother.

I had exposed Bellamont a Black Hand Operative as a traitor. I was awarded a Cowl and promoted to Speaker. Then I was magically teleported to Night Mother's resting place. I appeared beside the Lucky Lady statue. When I arrived, I couldn't move. Arquen recited an invocation and for a moment, the statue seemed to come to life. It revealed a hidden trap door down to the crypt of Night Mother.

After my companions descended, I could move again. I followed them. But not before activating the statue for some luck points.

After I descended, Bellamont attacked. He killed Alor and Belisarius on the spot. Then he came after me, but with Arquen's help, he went down.

After he was dead, the night mother spoke to me. She explained everything to me, and invited me to loot Bellamont's body for the Longsword of Burndif. Then she sent me back to the Cheydinhal Sanctuary.

Once I arrived, Arquen spoke to me and laid out everything, she told me that she was going to get the Sanctuary up and running again. I would serve as the Brotherhood's Listener, the conduit between the Speakers and the Night Mother.

I had reached the top of the Brotherhood's ladder.

I decided that it was time to go home for a while. I went back to the places that I had just been and picked up everything that I had left behind and sorted it all out by item type and I fenced it all, raking in $30,000 gold.

Then I slept and leveled up.

Next, it was time to deliver the Amulet of Kings to Jauffre. I went to Chorrol and made my way to the Weynon Lodge, after giving it to him I was invited inside.

I was approached to do a mission by Jauffre. He needed me to go get his illegitimate son Martin from the Chapel of Akatosh in the city of Kvatch. When I arrived, I met Hirtel who told me that Daedra had destroyed Kvatch. I was told by some others that Savlian Matius might know more. Matius told me that a few people were still alive and at the Chapel, including the priest.

CHAPTER 23

THE RESCUE OF MARTIN

I summoned all the Daedra that I could and went to work clearing the area. Inside first was Blood Feast, then Rendering Halls, then Corridors of Dark Salvation and then Sigillum Sanguis. When I got to Sigil Stone at the top of Sanguis, I was teleported back to Oblivion Gate with Matius.

Matius then asked me if I would help him liberate the city at the west end. There was myself, swordsmen Ilend Vonius and bowman Merandil and Jesaon Rilian.

When we had cleared the city, Matius asked me if I would like to become a blade. Matius told me that I could help myself to anything I needed and that he would get Martin for me.

Martin thanked me for coming to his rescue and I told him that I needed to take him back to Jauffre; the trek was long and uneventful.

When we got back to the Priory, it was under attack by Mythic Dawn Assassins.

It took a while to clean up. Then with Jauffre to run out to me to tell me that the amulet was missing.

I took Jauffre and Martin to Cloud Ruler Temple high in the Jerall

Mountains northwest of Bruma, where they'd be safe as the temple was well guarded by warrior priests.

When we got there a man named Cyrus invited us in.

I told Jauffre that I would be a Blade and I was eligible to use any and all armor in the Fortress Armory.

Jauffre told me to find a Blade Master named Baurus to help me. He was living in Luther Broad's Boarding House in the Elven Gardens. I gave stable hand Restita Statlilia a handful of gold to watch Shadowmare for me. I stuck out like a sore thumb when I entered the gardens because of the way that I was dressed.

I found Barus and he asked me to meet him at the sewers at midnight. There was no one around so we looted the whole place. I found four books magical discipline and one called Mehrunes to Dagon's Shrine which looked very interesting so I read it; and it taught me what I needed to know about going to the Dagon Shrine and what to do once I got there.

I knew that I needed to get some training.

I went to the Tomb of Prince Camarril in Green Emperor way and waited until noon for the glowing map to appear on the door. It marked the Mythic Dawn Shrine. I headed to Dagon Shrine near Lake Arrius.

When I got to the cave there was a man lying there who died by someone's hand and I searched his body and there was a key on him. I took out my bow and summoned some Daedra to help me in the caves. Soon, I found a priest named Jeelius lying wounded on the altar. I helped him and he ran off.

When I got back to the temple, I told Martin of the books, and gave them to him; he told me that it would take a while to study them.

Jauffre told me of strangers walking the roads. I set myself up to watch for them. I followed the pair of figures to a cave. Summoning some Daedra, I picked the lock and went in.

I found plans by Ruma Camoran to destroy the fortress and kill Martin. I made my way back to Martin and told him.

Ronald Knipfer

CHAPTER 24

THE DAEDRIC SHRINES

Time to do some Daedric Quests before I went to the Dagon Shrine.

First to Azura. Back to Jerall Mountains, I traveled to Lord Rugdumph's Estate then made my way to Azura's shrine. She needed me to have Glow Dust in my inventory, and I gave it to her and she asked me to relieve the suffering of five of her followers who were infected with Vampirism after killing the vampire Dratik. She told me to go to the Gutted Mine.

I did as she asked and returned to her and lit her candles and she gave me a Soul Gem called Azure's Star.

Then I was off to Boethia's Shrine, for him I needed a Daedra Heart. This God told me that I was not of his flock but I could prove it to him by killing off members of other races. He opened a portal. I accepted his challenge and after fulfilling my part of the bargain, he gave me a Splendid Enchanted Sword called "Goldbrand".

The next stop was Clavieus Vile, this Shrine needed $500 gold. I had to retrieve the sword Umbra she was Vindasel at an Ayleid ruin along the Red Ring Road. When I viewed Vindasel off in the distance I summoned 10 Spider Daedra and then cast a paralyzing spell on her and the spiders took off to attack her. Back at the Shrine, I declined to give him the sword, and I was praised.

The next one was Hircine. I had to offer the Shrine a Bear Pelt. This God wanted me to bring back a Unicorn Horn from Harcane Grove. Before the Unicorn, there were three Minotaurs. I slew the Minotaur's with ease and the Unicorn was not an easy fight. The God rewarded me with Savior's Hide.

Then came Malacath. This God wanted Troll Fat. This God asked me to free Ogre's from their enslavement. The Orge's were being forced to work in Bleak Mine. The guards standing over them were dark elves. I had to sneak in and I summoned ten ghosts while using my bow, I took out the guards and set the Ogre's free and made my way back to the Shrine where the God gave me The Great Hammer Volendrung.

Then it was off to Mephala's Shrine. This time I needed Nightshade. She told me to go to Bleaker's Wat where Dark Elves and Nord's lived side by side in harmony and to kill the leaders of each tribe, leaving evidence that the other tribe did the killing. After the deed was finished, I was rewarded with an Ebony Blade.

The next stop was the Shrine at Meridia west of Skingrad. This female God wanted bone meal. She wanted me to go to Howling Cave and kill all of the Necromancer's there. That was easy, I just summoned 20 Spider Daedra to fight with me, and we killed them, afterwards I looted their bodies and took everything that they had. The majority of what they had was Alchemy materials. Back at the Shrine, I was given the Ring of Khajiiti. The ring had "Chameleon" and "Fortify Speed" enchantments on it 20 points per.

The Shrine of Molag Bal was next on the list. This God wanted a Lion Pelt and then wanted me to go to Melus Petilius who had taken an oath of non-violence and induce him to attack me.

Petilius lived near Brindle Home. It was easy to convince him to attack me. I followed him to his wife's grave after 10:00 PM.

When I reappeared back at the Shrine I was given the Mace of Molag Bal.

My next Daedric quest was Namira; her shrine is southeast of Bruma. She told me of a group of worshippers who live in absolute darkness of the Ayleid ruin Anga. There were some do-gooder priests who were planning to shed light on them. I was to use Namira's Shroud and kill these do-gooders. When I returned to the Shrine Namira gave me a ring with "Reflect damage and Reflect spell enchantments.

Next was the Goddess Nocturnal located on the road that runs east from Upper Niben from Leyawiin. Nocturnal asked me to return the Eye of Nocturnal from the thieves at Tidewater Cave who has stolen it.

Tidewater cave was on the Topal Bay coast southeast of the city. When I returned from the job, I was given a skeleton key which was an unbreakable lockpick and it boosted my security skill by 40 points.

After this I went to Peryite on the southeast bank of the Silverfish River east of the Imperial Bridge Inn. She told me that some of her followers have cast a spell that separated their souls from their bodies and she wanted me to help them. I was rewarded with a shield called Spell Breaker with a strong Reflect Spell enchantment.

Then it was off to see Sanguine southwest of the Weatherlash Estate. This shrine was in need of Cyrodiilic Brandy. I was given a Daedra summoning staff called The Sanguine Rose.

Sheogorath was my next stop; it was near the border a little less than half-way between Bravil and Leyawiin. This shrine was in need of Lettuce, a Lesser Soul Gem and Yarn. I had to go to Border Watch and make a most dire prophecy come true. I had to go to town and ask about the "K'Sharra Prophecy" and my cover was that I was a traveling scholar.

At the Vaermina Shrine southwest of Cheydinhal on the east shore of Lake Poppad. This shrine got a Grand Black Soul Gem from me. I was asked to retrieve the stolen Orb of Vaermina from the tower of Wizard Arkved southeast of her shrine. I was given the Skull of Corruption for a job well done.

The Jerall Mountains were next on my list. Mora asked me to collect 10 souls; one from each race. After this job I was given a spell book. I was asked to choose Steel, Shadow or Spirit. Steel offered me combat. Shadow offered me stealth, and Spirit offered me magic. I didn't know what steel or spirit offered me as I did not take it, instead I chose Shadow. Shadow gave me speed, acrobatics, light armor, security and sneak by 10 points each.

I went back to the guild and put the rewards I wanted to keep in a chest. I went to Martin and asked him about Daedra artifacts and he wanted me to go to Sancre Tor and retrieve the armor of Tiber Septim and bring it back to him.

There were some dart traps that he had set up. I came across a lever that opened a gate in front of me. I came face to face with the undead Reilus; he left me the Amulet of Ansel after he died. Then it was on to the Entry Hall and Hall of Judgment. After I finally found the Tomb of Reman Emperor the undead warriors were kneeling in front of the armor and let me take it.

Then Martin sent me off to find the Great Weylnd Stone from Miscanand an Ayleid Ruin. Sel Vauna led me to a Varla stone which recharged all of my weapons; then to Morimath.

I was told by Jauffre that I had to go to Bruma and help close the Oblivion Gate. When I got there I told Captain Burd to tell his men when they saw me enter the Citadel to leave.

I put on my Jak Boots and jumped up to the roof of the citadel. Then down to the steps, up the levels to the Rending Halls. I grabbed the Sigil Stone and it teleported me outside Burma. Then it was to the

Oblivion Gate outside Chorrol; another Sigil Stone and another teleportation. I then went to Leyawiin and did this all over Cyrodiil.

My next quest was to defend the city of Bruma. I went to all of the great Castles of all the great cities asking for soldiers to take up arms with me.

I summoned 10 of every creature that I had spells for and made my way to the World-Breaker. Inside I found a Dremora Sigil Keeper who held a key to the upper levels. After killing him I took his key to Vaults of the End of Times and found a door to the World-Breaker and another Dremora with a key around his neck at the top of the tower the Sigillum Sanguis there was an army of Dremora Markynaz's waiting for me. After killing them and grabbing the stone I was teleported back to Bruma.

Making my way back to Martin he told me that this was the last ingredient in creating the portal.

I rested and leveled up again.

I repaired all of my armor and weapons and gathered more arrows.

I entered the portal and found myself standing in a white stone enclosure.

Heading east, I came across a Dremora who told me to either defeat or free the Xivilai Anazes.

His lair was north by northwest. Once inside I came across three ascended immortals who told me the story of their imprisonment. I freed the Xivilai Anazes and he thanked me after kill the immortals.

I returned the way I came and then headed to Carac Agaialor then to where Mankar Camoran was and killed him and his two children.

1 was then teleported back to the Cloud Ruler Temple and gave the Amulet of Kings to Martin.

After a day of rest, I went to see Countess Narina Carvain who told me that she collected Akaviri artifacts...

CHAPTER 25

SENTINEL STATUE

First it was off to Dragonclaw Rock and west up the hill to the Sentinel Statue and then north to the Serpent's Trail. Then I came to a dungeon that was full of Ogres and nasty creatures; the door at the end of the passage to me led to a hidden valley.

I had to reach the commander Mishaxhi in the Venom of the Serpent Level. Holding the orders from the skeleton in the dungeon Mishaxhi thought I was the courier from the Akaviri homeland. He talked to me and then got up and walked into a wall and vanished. A secret door came to life revealing a treasure vault. The Madstone was on a pedestal, the side door was a shortcut to Scales of the Serpent. I took the Madstone and went back to Countess Narina Carvain who gave me the Ring of the Vipereye which had Fortify Agility and Resist Magic enchantments.

There were four concealed containers. Three of them with keys and the last held a potent magic ring.

From the tower that held the entrance to the Pale Pass Fort I descended the path to a frozen lake.

I made my way to the destroyed fortress. Up against some rocks next to a big mushroom I saw a barrel, inside a crumpled note and a rusty key. The note told the story of the theft of a ring.

There was a second tower west of the one I just left. I found a bush with a chest under it, in the chest was an "Old Key".

Making my way I found a chest containing a "Forgotten Key". Still searching the area I found the "Circle of Omnipotence" which boosted my Agility, Endurance, Speed, Strength, and Willpower by 3 points each.

My next quest after a day's rest took me to a hidden cavern near Chorrol behind a waterfall that was called "Black Rock Caverns". This was a quest of disappearing rocks and turning handles. There were several bandits and some pirates and an old pirate ship. Entering in the cavern while in sneak, and summoning 20 ghosts, I searched the cavern very carefully. In the big room on the second level, I turned a handle that was hidden behind some rocks against the southeast wall near the south corner. All it appeared to do was close a door in the southwest wall that led back to one of the two entrances to the first level. When I returned to the top level, there were two Black Rock Pirates, a bowman, and a melee fighter; they materialized on a rise to my right. I shot one with a paralyze spell, and the ghosts attacked them all. After a while the three pirates were dead.

Once I had killed the bad men, I checked out the area where they had been. There used to be some rocks there and now a handle had appeared in its place. I turned the handle and nothing happened. When

I returned to the big room there was now a trap door where a big rock had been.

The trap door led down to "Lost Black Rock Chasm". There was a trail of skeletons, and dead bandits down to a dead end. There was a handle on the right hand wall that when pulled, was used to remove the rock that was blocking the way to an old pirate ship. I looted the place to my heart's content. I found that there was more than I could carry, so I had to cast "Fortify Strength" on myself ten more times bringing my strength up to 3000, and then I could carry everything that I wanted.

I took all the treasure from the Pirate's ship to my house and unloaded everything.

Asking around about anything new happening that needed attention, I heard about some trouble with goblins. I had to travel along the Yellow Road from the Imperial City till I came to the Corbolo River and when I came to a small camp at Crestbridge I found a man named Barthel who told me of his problem.

They wanted to settle up at Cropsford but they were chased off because of a Goblin War Party. I told Barthel I would take care of his problem. One tribe of goblins was based out of Timberscare Hollow (the Rock Biter Goblins) and the other out of Cracked Wood Cave (the Bloody Hand Goblins). Killing both tribes was nothing. Went back to Barthel and told him that he could settle where he wanted.

Next I went to the Barren Mine; south of the mouth of the Panther River. There was a tribe of Goblins who called themselves "The Dust Easters." Then I went to the Derelict Mine and then the Plundered Mine.

1 made my way to the Wenderbek Cave I took the Totem I had collected then to Goblin Jim and was able to give it to him in peace. I was given the name Kawhatcha.

Then it was on to kill the Highwaymen. To kill each of the highwaymen, I cast a paralyze spell and cast 10 Lichs. By casting the paralyze spell, I allowed the Lichs to do the dirty work.

Chorrol Side of Fort Ash road.

The North End of Yellow Road Bridge.

The middle of Long Red Road Bridge across the Upper Niben off of Lake Rumare.

The last was on the Gold Road north of Anvil at the turn off of Lord Drad's Estate.

I went back to the Mage's Guild in Bravil to buy some more spells from Kud-Ei. Kud-Ei needed my help to find a missing friend. I asked Kud-Ei to accompany me to where her friend was last seen. She took me to a home where she knelt down next to a man lying on a cot and told me that his mind was gone. I lay on the bed next to her friend and using an amulet and she put me to sleep while I was looking for her friend. I walked around found some sphere of energy and fought two Minotaurs and after picking up the energy spheres, I found myself back in bed.

Kud-Ei told me that an Arch-Mage didn't need to pay for spells, but I convinced her to make a profit off of me, and she agreed to sell me any spell for $100 gold each.

I had heard through the rumor mill that Arnora Aurai needed some help recovering some money that was stolen from her boyfriend Jorundr. I ran to Bruma and quickly located her house on the south side of the city.

She told me that she had unwillingly served as an accomplice in some of Jorundr crimes. She also told me that Jorundr had killed a guard during the commission of one of his crimes. She had returned to their hideout to find that the gold had been moved and she wanted me to go to the prison and visit Jorundr and find out from him what he had done with the gold.

I pick pocketed a guard and chose jail so that I could be jailed with Jorundr and he told me that Arnora had killed the guard and blamed it on him. He told me that he wanted her dead and that if I brought him her amulet he would tell me where he hid the gold.

1 paid my fine and was released.

I went to a guard and told him that Arnora was the one who killed the guard and told him of a plan to trap Arnora.

1 went to Arnora and told her that Jorundr wanted to see her dead and that if I brought him the amulet he would tell me where the gold is. I told her that if she would let me borrow her amulet I would take her to the gold.

I took the amulet to Jorundr and he told me where the gold is, and I went back to Arnora and told her and there was a guard waiting for her when she got there.

I then went to talk to Llevana Nedaren at her house just south of the Great Chapel of Stendarr. She needed to bring charges against her boss. His name was Lerland, and I went to him and told him that if he didn't go talk to Llevana he was going to go to jail for a long time. He went and the next thing I heard he was being led away from her house in handcuffs.

1 next went to Skingrad and talked to court steward Hal-Liurz about purchasing Redthron Hall, however he sent me to Sham gro-Yang the Count's butler. I gave him some gold and flattered him and raised his disposition and asked him if I could purchase his house, I gave him $25,000 gold and he gave me the key.

In the cellar I found an hourglass with five flawless diamonds, three flawless emeralds, two flawless sapphires, and the Ring of the Gray.

The ring fortified my Sneak, Marksman, Security and Acrobatics +5 along with a Resistance to Poison and Detect Life as well.

Talking to people, I heard about a wayward knight near Cheydinhal. When I got there I found that the Oblivion gate had opened and there was a guard patrolling the area. I approached him and asked him what happened and he told me that that Count Andel Indary's son Farwil and six of his men had gone missing. The Count is offering a reward for the return of his son or confirmation of his death.

I told the guard that I would go in and find the Count's son. I went in and found three knights lying dead, and I looted their bodies. Further investigation towards the southeast of the gate led me to Farwil and I told him that his father wanted him to return home. He told me that he had to close the gate. I told him to go home and that I would close the gate. He insisted on going with me to see that it was done.

As we advanced towards the gate it opened of its own accord, and we continued on and the next gate opened for us as well. As we entered the Citadel we fought at least a dozen Daedra and Dremora. We fought our way to the Rendering Halls which held more Daedra and then onto the Corridors of Dark Salvation.

I had to offer the knights healing as we went along to keep them alive it was a tough battle. When we made it to the top I spotted the Sigil Stone with a Daedra Boss. I summoned a few creatures to help out with the battle and the knights, Farwil and I used our bows against this monster and he was down in no time.

I told everyone to hold onto me as I reached for the stone and after I touched the stone we all were transported to safety outside of Oblivion gate and we all watched it close and disappear. Farwil then honored me with the title Knight of the Thom. I was given a medallion that held a Speechcraft enchantment X 10.

We then returned to the Count's and he gave me a choice of two weapons: Thornblade which held the Disintegrate Armor enchantment; and the Staff of Indary's which held Damage Strength and Shock Damage enchantments. I chose the staff.

I then took off for Chorrol to visit the Chorrol Castle and see if I could get some training in Destruction.

I soon heard a rumor about Reynald Jemane, and I asked around and no one had heard of Reynald but they knew a Guilbert Jemane. It turned out they were twins who did not know of each other. I had to arrange a meeting.

I found out that there home had three Ogres living in it and I had to dispatch the Ogres for the twins.

It was time to head home for a good night's sleep and to make some potions and repair my armor and get some more arrows.

I went to the Mages Guild and Fathis Ules told me that Jemane's father Albert was a professional thief who worked for the Thieves guild but had kept something for himself after one of the assignments. He may have hidden at Weatherleah. Ules however thought that the Ogres may have taken the item to Redguard Valley Cave.

It took me awhile and some summoning and some spell casting to rid the cave of goblins and Ogres but I found the Honorblade of Chorrol and I returned the blade to the Castle where the Royal Steward Laythe Wavrick told me that sword had indeed been stolen. He gave me as a reward an Escutcheon of Chorrol which is a shield with Fortify Endurance and Reflect Damage enchantments on it.

I heard about a Necromancer Lair hidden in a trench east of the Silverfish River and northwest of Lake Canulus. I'll get there someday.

CHAPTER 26

THE SEARCH OF AYLEID RUINS

I then decided it was time to check out some of the Ayleid ruins for lost statues. The first was the Franacas ruins which held Vampires.

The next ruin I went to was Mackamentain which is to the south of Nibenay Basin.

I needed some sleep so for safety, I went to the Bloated Float Inn and when I awoke in the morning a porter named Lynch was waiting for me. I killed him and upon searching his body I found a key to a storage room and some instructions. I went to the storage room and found Graman gro-Marad there. He told me about a ship and that if I helped him he would be able to get the ship into port.

When I got to the ship I met Minx and told Minx that Lynch had sent me to help Selene. Minx told me that Selene was in Ormil's cabin and I killed her. I found a key on her. I took the key and found a Wraith on the rear deck. He had the key to Ormil's on his dead body. Going to Ormil's I convinced Selene to surrender to me.

Castle Leyawiin and Count Marius Caro for work. He told me that if I was interested in joining the Knights of White Stallion that there were some Black Bow bandits that needed taken care of that were operating out of Ayleid Ruins called Te'lepe. The boss was named Brugo and that I could take Mazoga along with me for support if I wanted to. While I was there I found a coffer and a note.

When we were done and had returned to Leyawiin the Count rewarded us and when I showed him the note he offered me a key to the White Stallion lodge.

Before I left Mazoga told me of a place where Black Bows go to fight. She led me to Rockmilk Cave across from Fisherman's Rock. I entered the cave and heard a fight and I killed everyone I came across. Eventually I found Mazoga lying dead. I collected about two dozen bows when I was done. When I brought the bows back to Caro I was tempted to keep the boss's bow as it was bigger and better than any of the others.

I went to Anvil and checked around with the townspeople and found out about the Chapel of Dibella, when I got there I found that everyone had been killed. I went to the Prophet across the street from the Chapel and he told me that I needed to go to the Shrine of the Crusader.

I wasn't going alone so I went to the Sanctuary and recruited a female Wood Elf named Carwen and went to the Mage's Guild and recruited a male Breton named Arcady Donat and told them to meet me at my house at 6 AM and we were going to have an adventure.

We went to the Niben River and the Vanua Exterior and I had them watch for me, and I went in. After a couple of battles with Wraiths, I called to them for help. There were a few skeleton guardians.

We made it to a huge room and I found the remains of Sir Amiel who held a key and a journal and a ring. There was a Knight of the Nine shield and a Helm, and a sword.

I turned to my comrades and told them to leave the way we came and we swam back to shore mounted our horses and went to the Priory.

In the cellar of the Chapel there was a circle made of eight diamonds with one in the middle, and in the northwest corner a door. Entering the door I was confronted by eight dead knights and the ghost of Sir Amiel who told me that I had to prove my worth by besting the eight dead knights.

I donned the ring of Sir Amiel and attacked these once brave knights killing them swiftly again. Once I had defeated them all I was given the: Gauntlets of the Crusader, Mace of the Crusader, Shield of the Crusader, and Boots of the Crusader. Sir Amiel told me to go to the opposite wall and to hold out the hand that wore his ring and when I did a niche opened revealing the Cuirass of the Crusader.

Sir Amiel told me that I need to go to the Underpall Cave. I mentioned this to Lathon a knight at the Priory and he agreed that I needed to go. I gathered my two companions and made for the cave. There were skeletal archers, a zombie and two skeleton heroes and a skeleton fighter. We went through the south wing, the north wing and came to

Reflecting Chamber. A wraith held the sword that we came for. And it was back to the Priory. I bid my companions farewell.

CHAPTER 27

THE FORLORN WATCHMAN

I went to go see my old friend Martin at the Cloud Ruler Temple. He told me that I should go talk to Gilgondorin at the Silverhome-on-the-Waterwill in Bravil. So I went there. He told me of the Forlorn Watchman. I had to go to a small island southeast of Bravil. There would be a watchman who wouldn't speak to me. I should follow him to a point on the hill just behind Fort Irony and he would tell me that he was the man once known as Grantham Blakely.

I went to the island and waited around. About 8PM a ghost appeared to me. I followed him until he introduced himself to me and told me that I had to look for his body "In the mouth of the Panther" then he looked across the bay to the southeast.

I went back to Gilgondorin and he showed me a book on the "Forlorn Watchman" and I found out that Grantham was using a metaphor for the Panther River.

I then swam across the river and found a cargo ship called the "Emma May" and it appeared to have run up on the rocks. I found a gaping hole in the side of the ship. After I cleaned the ship out of various monsters Grantham appeared to me again.

I then headed off to the Grey Mare Inn in Chorrol and was met by

Valis Odiil who asked if I had seen his sons Rallus and Antus. He told me that they wanted him and asked if I would go in his place and I found them and we went back to their farm where I did battle with some goblins who had been terrorizing their place. I was rewarded with a sword called Chillrend.

On my way back to Chorrol I ran into Dar-Ma. After returning to Chorrol, I made my way to the Mage's guild for a good night's sleep, then going to check on Dar-Ma. Dar-Ma's mother told me that she had went on an errand and was long overdue. She had been going to a small village called Hackdirt. I went into Moslin's Dry Goods and found a trap door and when I picked the lock I found a mine and Dar-Ma being held in a cage. Her mother awarded me +5 to my Mercantile Skills.

I needed to buy a spell from the Temple District in Imperial City called Superior Convalescence and wanted to modify it. While there I met with a woman named Ralso Norvala and she beseeched me to come meet her husband Gilem and a man named Seridur at her house. After I bought the spell, I went with her.

CHAPTER 28

THE VAMPIRE HUNTERS

Once there I met a group of men who called themselves the Order of Virtuous Blood, that they were a group of vampire hunters. Seridur stepped forward and told me that they had found a vampire in their midst a man named Roland Jenseric, he had been seen struggling with a woman and they wanted me to kill him.

I went to Jenseric's and he told me that he was no vampire that Seridur was the true vampire. I went back and told Seridur that the deed was done and he gave me a reward and then when I got him alone, I cast my Daylight spell on him and he burst into flames.

I collected his ashes and went to the Order and told them the truth and they gave me The Ring of Sunfire which held Reflect Spell and Resist Disease on it.

I then heard of a rumor about several merchants in the Market District complaining about unfair practices. I went there and found a merchant at the "Good as New" shop by the name of Jensine and she implored me to follow the Wood Elf Thorinor of the Copious Coinpurse. He closed his store at 9PM and about 11PM he made his way to a small garden where he was met by a Nord Agarmir. I then followed the Nord to his home and waited until he left again. When he did, I picked the lock to his home and found a book called "Macabre Manifest" which listed people's names and jewelry they were wearing.

I went back to Jensine and told her about the book and she wanted to help me. I went to the palace graveyard and found the entrance to the Trentius Family Mausoleum had been unsealed. Killing the Nord I found a sword on him called Debaser and a mace with enchantments. I went back to Jensine and she gave me the Weatherward Circlet a ring with Resist Frost and Resist Fire.

I went to Leyawiin Mage's Guild to pick up another spell. As I entered the Guild all eyes were upon me and I began receiving praise for becoming the new Arch-Mage. Everyone was eager to help me, as I needed the spell Produce Heat. While everyone was looking for it, one mage S'drassa approached me. He needed my help as my reputation as an adventurer had become quite high. He needed to know if I could collect some crystals "Garridan's Tears" for him, they were the frozen blue tears of the Knight Garridan Starrous. He told me that if I were to need more information for them to go see Julienne Fanis at the Arcane University.

I went to go see Fanis and she told me to go to the "First Edition Book Store" and locate the book "Knightfall". The book told me that I needed refined Frost Salts to enter the region. I went back to Fanis to see if she could tell me where to purchase some and sure enough she had some herself.

I needed to go to Frostfire Glade because the cold at the center of the Glade was extremely intense. The circlet that I owned was enough to protect me from the cold. However, the book also mentioned "Philter of Frostward" and Fanis sent me back to S'drassa for that.

I had to go to the caves southeast of Bruma. Entering Frostfire Cave I made sure that I had the ring on. There were rats and bears all over the cave. Just north of the entrance Garridan and a Frost Atronach were locked forever in a frozen embrace. There was a Frost Atronach defending the sculpture and after his defeat I found the five tears around the base of the sculpture.

I cast the "Light Me on Fire" spell on the glades as I was leaving. I returned to S'drassa with the tears and my reward.

CHAPTER 29

SHERINA

Then I decided to go see Sherina at the Leyawiin Fighter's Guild to see if there were any jobs for me to do but then people around me began telling me about foul odors coming from Rosenita Gallenius's house.

When I entered her home she was holding the "Staff of Everscamp" a trick played by Daedric Lord Sheogorath. I went back to the mage's guild to ask for help in getting rid of the scamps and Alves Uvenim told me that I had to willingly accept the staff and return it to Sheogorath's Shrine in Darkfathom Cave.

I took the staff back to the shrine and had to fight a dozen Daedra before leaving, after killing them, I took all their swords and sold each of them for $25,000 gold, which gave me $300,000 gold.

When I went back to Rosenita's she rewarded me with the Ring of Gidolon's Edge which held Block and Blade skill enchantments +5.

I then learned that Wawnet Inn was in need of help. So I went there and the owner told me that she collected wine but had been unable to collect the Shadowbanish Wine. The only place that she knew it to be was in the Imperial Legion Forts. She asked me to bring her six bottles and she would reward me well. The eight places I needed to go were

Fort Aurus, Fort Carmala, Fort Dirich, Fort Grief, Fort Irony, Fort Magia, Fort Scinia, and Fort Vlastarus. It took me awhile but it was well worth the reward to collect for her the six bottles that she needed.

As I was leaving she asked me if I was willing to help someone else.

A fisherman named Aelwin Merowald needed my help. She said that he had been bitten by a Slaughterfish and was out of commission for a little while. So I went to his home and he told me that he needed 12 Rumare Slaughterfish scales to fulfill a contract. He told me that I should go to northwest part of Lake Rumare. These weren't just ordinary Slaughterfish these were Tamriel Barracuda. It took me about an hour to acquire what he needed. He gave me the "Jewel of Rumare" a ring with Fortify Athletics and Water Breathing enchantments.

Walking about I had heard about a vampire named Kindrail (Hindaril) who was east of the Panther River in Redwater Slough. I went there to defeat him with my daylight spell.

I then began to hear tales of Uderfrykte Matron the meanest and deadliest creature in all of the land. A beggar told me that I needed to go to Aerin's Camp first. Near the camp I found the body of Andre Labouche. In his pocket was a letter mentioning the creature known as the Horror of Dive Rock. Dive Rock is the pinnacle of the Northeast.

On the mountain's slope I found an empty campsite with "Agnar's Journal". While there I was able to see all of Northeast Cyrodiil. This added locations to my map. I went back to the gully and followed it southeast until I found the creature and on its corpse I found the Frostwyrm Bow with a Frost Damage enchantment.

I went back to Bruma and asked around if anyone needed any help and found a guard standing outside the home of Bradon Lirrian who told me the home had become a crime scene. I raised his disposition to 70 and he told me that Bradon may be a vampire and that two corpses had been found in shallow graves and that a third had been found in his cellar. Vampire hunter Raynil Dralas had come to town about this time. Bradon's wife Erline insisted her husband was not a vampire. I decided that there was nothing that I could do and decided to go to Olav's Tap and Tuck for a good night's sleep.

I spotted a journal out of the corner of my eye just as I was about to lie down and decided that after a good night's sleep, I would read it in the morning. So, I put it in my inventory and went to sleep. The journal recounted the exploits of Gelebourne, Bradon and Raynil of an Ayleid Ruin. They were able to retrieve a potent artifact.

I went to Olav and he told me that Gelebourne was the previous vampire that Raynil had been hunting. There were some keys that needed to be retrieved from them. So I took the journal to the guard and he sent me to Boreal Stone cave and so I did and beat Raynil in a battle that shook the cave. I took the three keys and opened a nearby chest and found an amulet. I took the amulet to Bradon's widow who spoke over it and it transformed into the Phylactery of Lithness.

CHAPTER 30

THE SEARCH FOR RYTHE

Around Bravil I heard that Ursanne Loche's husband Aleron was missing. She told me that her husband was a gambler and was in debt to an Ore named Kurdan gro-Dragol. She told me that her husband was to meet Kurdan the day before at Lonely Suitor Lodge and had never come home. So I went to the lodge and the owner told me that if I wanted to find out about Aleron I needed to go to Grief Island out on Niben Bay and retrieve his father's axe.

I took a boat out to the ruins and inside was Aleror Loche and there were traps and gates and keys that all took my time to get to the center of Hunter's Abyss. When I got back to shore I went to Ursanne and told her about her husband's death and she gave me a book, "Biography of the Wolf Queen".

When I got to Cheydinhal a woman came running up to me to tell me about her husband Rythe going missing. She told me that he was a great painter and that he had vanished from a locked room. She gave me a key and took me to his room, inside there was nothing suspicious then when I touched the painting I was transported inside. I walked around the forest and found Rythe who told me that a Bosmer had attacked him and entered the painting with his Brush of Truepaint. I found the brush and went back to Rythe who took us to the south until he painted a door and we were back in his studio. He gave me the "Apron of Adroitness" as a reward which was enchanted to boost my Intelligence and Agility by 10 points each.

In the Temple District I was told of a corrupt guard who had shaken down Jensine, I was told that Luronk gro-Glurzog and Raslan were the thieves. Jensine told me that it was Audens Avidius who was the thief. I went to Glurzog and Raslan and got them to agree to speak to Hayn in the morning and they did. They went to confront Avidius and he issued a threat against me as he was led off to jail.

Outside the gate of the Imperial Prison a guard named Lerexus Callidus told me of a Skooma dealer, the leader of the gang was a Dark Elf named Kylius Lonavo. He told me to go to his home South by Southwest of where we were. I went to the house and obliterated everyone inside and found Lonavo's ring in what was left of the mess I made and I took it back to the guard as proof of the deed.

On the Green Road, just near the headwaters of the White River I met up with a Khajiit who told me that someone had run off with her potatoes. And they had run into the woods. It was an Ogre, I killed him and took the potatoes back to the poor woman and she offered me five loaves of bread.

Then I heard that Malene at the Roxey Inn on the Red Ring Road in the Northeast corner of Lake Rumare wanted help. He told me that Raelynn the Gravefinder must die, since Raelynn moved into the Moss

Rock Cavern it was no longer safe to walk in the woods. After I killed Raelynn, I went back to Malene who told me that there was a bear problem at Shardrock.

Thorley Aethelred told me that bears had been attacking his flock. I found bears to the north, east of the pond, and to the south and the southwest. I took the fangs to Thorley and he showed me seven books and told me that I could have one.

Just outside the ruined city of Kvatch lies Shetcombe Farm. Inside I found the page of a journal belonging to a Slythe Seringi who had written about "The Sunken One" in nearby Sandstone Cavern. The cave was just northwest of the farm. Inside the cave were many enemies. I fought my way through the cave swinging my blade and letting arrows fly and killing every beast inside. I collected all of my fallen enemies' weapons and took them with me.

I came across the village of Aleswell near the junction of the Silver Road crossing the road to Bruma. It seemed that everyone had become invisible. I was told to talk to Diram Serethi at the Inn. He told me that wizard Ancotar had done this but he had gone missing. He was last seen at Fort Caractacus. I went to Caractacus and found it empty as well. Searching the place I found Ancotar's journal and discovered that he had become upset that the residents of Aleswell were complaining about him. I cast a detect life spell and found the wizard in the fort and admonished him for his work and demanded that he return everyone to normal and he gave me a scroll and a ring. He told me to go to the center of town to cast the spell.

I then went to Count Regulus Terentiusd.

"I would like to buy your home."

"How much are you willing to give me for it?"

"I will pay whatever you ask."

"How does $100,000 gold sound to you?"

"It sounds like a fair price to me."

"Well then, the house is yours for the taking."

"I really appreciate the deal. Thank you for the house."

I went to Quill-Weave and found her sitting alone.

"Ma'am, I would like to hire you for a job if you are willing."

"What do you have in mind, son?"

"Well, I just bought a house, and I need someone to watch over the place for me, while I am traveling about the country-side."

"What do you need this old lady for?"

"You see, I trust you and I think that you are the perfect candidate for me."

"What are you asking me to do?"

"I need someone, to not only keep the place lived in, but I need someone to protect my belongings."

"What do you want to pay me?"

"I will start off at $25 gold a month, plus a place to stay and all the food that you can eat, and training in any skill that you would like to learn. I will even help you cross-class train by paying for your lessons."

"Sounds like you really want me to help you with this."

"You bet; I really want you to take this job, so I have made the offer as sweet as I can for you."

"You have a deal."

I went back to Imperial City and found that Christophe had been looking for me.

"A portal has recently appeared just south of Leyawiin. I think that you should go check it out."

"Sounds interesting."

"It could get you back home."

I headed off to the portal and found out that it was just a gate to Oblivion. So I headed back to Christophe.

"I need you to hold onto some stuff for me."

"Sure thing."

"Thank you."

I took only the essentials that I needed and left the rest with him.

"If I don't return you can have everything that I am leaving with you. If not, and this is a test, I'll be back."

"I'll be here waiting for your return."

"I appreciate all that you have done for me, and you have been a good friend."

"I hope to see you again."

"I'm sure that we will meet again."

CHAPTER 31

OBLIVION COMES CALLING

I returned to Leyawiin and entered the gate. Inside there was lava everywhere but I had to make it to the center cathedral, fighting my way through Daedra and all kinds of crap. When I got to the cathedral and entered the building that is when the big battle began. And for someone having 3000 strength, I killed everything quickly. Gathered up as many weapons as possible headed for the top of the cathedral and grabbed the sigil stone. With a flash of light I was back outside the gate. I then traveled to my new house that I had just bought from Count Regulus Terentiusd.

I repaired all of the weapons and left them there. And then went to see Christophe, and let him know that I was alive and well. He then told me that gates have been opening up all over the place, and he thought I should check them out.

Leyawiin was safe, and I went to Burma to see if there was a gate there and there was. My first thing was to get healed, pick up some grand healing spells, check my weapons and armor and entered the gate. Inside it was the same thing as Leyawiin. I fought my way through collecting weapons as I went and headed for the sigil stone, which I grabbed a hold of and it teleported me outside the gate. Like before, I traveled to my new house and repaired all of the weapons and dropped them off.

This continued all over the country repeatedly, and by the time that I was done everything was back to normal. I collected well over 2090 pounds of weapons, and I took them to the house, to repair them and saw that they were all gone but a bag had appeared on a shelf, and when I looked in the bag there they all were. I repaired the weapons that I had just brought with me, and left them on the floor.

Looking at each weapon, including the ones that were in the bag, gave me a selling price of over $3 million in gold. So, if I wanted to I could buy better weapons and armor by selling the weapons that I had.

My next goal was to find the spell Sanctuary. Using it with soul trap, and casting it on myself would make me a Superman.

Plus I always had a knack for collecting Grand Soul Gems casting a soul trap on a higher being and trapping that being's soul in the gem and finally using that soul to enchant a new weapon.

I walked away to make a lot of gold.

Some friends who I had met while in Anvil had invited me to go with them on a fishing trip in their luxury yacht. I decided to go with them as I hadn't been fishing in a long time. I thought it would be a great idea for me to get away and relax. I had never been fishing in this world and it would be a brand new experience for me. The Captain of the boat was Nijal and he was married to a wonderful woman named

Salene, and they had a cook Jern. It was just the four of us. We had left port in the early morning hours and it was a beautiful day out on the sea. The sea was calm and serene; the boat rocked back and forth in the waves and it was like a cradle rocking to put a baby to sleep. The wind was light and cool. It was enough to fill the sail but not enough to put any speed into the craft.

The water was clear and blue with a hint of green. The lines were cast and the fish were nibbling. No one had caught a bite all day.

Sometime after the noon meal and we were taking a break from the fishing, I was pacing the deck and enjoying the view and the weather. While I was pacing the deck, I heard someone yell, "Abandon Ship!" I couldn't tell whether it was Nijal or Jern but it was a loud yell. I ran back to the stern to see what was happening. Everybody had gone. The wheel had been tied to keep the boat on a course to the open seas.

I saw a shimmer of light in the distance. It grew closer as each minute passed. I was in a panic as Nijal, his wife and Jern had disappeared. What was I to do? I had no idea where I was and the knot was unfamiliar to me. I couldn't turn the boat away from the shimmering light as it grew closer.

I realized why they had left, but why didn't they wait for me? Why did they leave the boat instead of trying to steer away from it? Where was I going to go? Where are they? I couldn't see them anywhere in the distance. I couldn't see them, and if I was going to jump, I would be in the middle of the open ocean with all kinds of dangerous fish in the water. I would be some animal's lunch for sure.

My only option was to stay aboard and sail through the light.

I awoke only to find myself standing on a rock near a pond that was surround by rocks, and a cliff, and this small oasis was in the middle of nowhere, meaning the area was surrounded uninhabited land.

The rock that I was on was really small it was about the size of a standard bed. I thought, "Oh shit, what the hell is this? Things like this don't happen to me twice."

Looking around me, I saw that a small wooden chest about the size of a shoebox was sitting on the edge of the rock, and next to it was a type of duffel bag that was made out some kind of cloth that seemed to be full. I could see the glimmer of the edge of a blade beneath the bag, and what looked like a staff was beside the blade.

So, sitting down on the rock I reach down to pick up the small chest to see what was inside. I found the chest to be locked and thought that the key might be in the bag. I reached over to pull the bag to me and as it slid it uncovered a long silver sword and what I had thought to be a staff turned out to be a long bow. It was a beautiful sword. It was engraved with strange yet beautiful designs. The artwork must have taken the craftsman hours to smith the blade and then engrave it. The bow however, was made of a wood that I wasn't familiar with. I had never seen the texture or the grain before. It was a striking bow. The wood was of an amber hue, and there were gems embedded in the wood. The string was similar to a fine horse hair. The wrappings were tight and the pull must have been about 65 pounds. It was a good sturdy bow that surely cost the owner greatly.

I then opened the bag to rummage through it for the key. Inside the bag, there was a quiver with about 30 arrows in it. I found several pieces of metal that had notches on the ends of them. I found a couple of knives, and there were bottles of various substances. I thought that one of the pieces of metal might jimmy the lock and open the chest.

I used the impromptu tool and there was a click, and presto, the chest was open to reveal either the biggest diamond I had ever seen or a very large paperweight.

I put the diamond inside my new shirt that was made out of leather, and I closed the chest and put it in the bag. I looked down at myself to see what all I was wearing as I noticed that when I was going to put the diamond away that my clothes had changed. I found myself to be wearing an outfit made out of leather.

My pants, boots, and shirt which happened to have a hood on it were all made of the finest leather that I had ever seen. The stitching was remarkable. The leather had polish to it. The boots were sturdy, as I stood back up to test them. They were almost knee high. There were additional bracings across the front. The soles were made of stiff leather; they appeared to be brand new as they had no scuff marks on them. The pants were snug without being tight; I could squat in them quite easily. I sat down with my legs crossed and using only the strength of my legs I was able to stand without any stress from the pants.

I hadn't noticed before but now that I was paying attention to my garments, I found myself to be wearing a fine leather shirt that had no pockets, but a hood instead of a collar. The room that it gave me to move around in was simple.

The scabbard for the sword was in the bag; I put the sword into it and slung the scabbard over my shoulder. I decided to carry the bow on my back next to the sword.

By the type and style of clothes that I was wearing, I began to assume that the gods, fates, or whomever had created a thief, with some fighting skills. All I remember from before this rock is the boat, and my name, everything else is a clean slate. Rudimentary skills are all I can grasp.

In front of me is a small pond that is about twenty feet across. At my back is a set of cliffs, these cliffs are three to four feet high with a rocky face. They could be climbable if I so dared.

There appeared to be a shrine near me that was made of bronze and stood five feet high and were various faces of the same god, but I would not know this until later.

There was a book lying next to the faces, it was called '2920 Midyear Volume 6'. What a strange title, I thought. I put it in the bag with the rest of my new belongings.

I began heading east and I soon came to a small clearing with a stack of stones that were standing as a column and flat on the top.

As I was inspecting these stones, I heard a noise behind me and I turned to find three medium creatures attacking me. Having good reflexes I quickly grabbed my sword and laid them to rest. These creatures had the ability to restore life to themselves and I had to dispatch all of them two more times each. I inspected them closer to find that I recognized them as a creature known as Spriggans.

I realized that the powers that brought me had given me the knowledge that I needed to be able to survive. What I needed would most likely come to me as I needed it and not before.

These stones seemed to have no real purpose; they were just a pile of stones that someone had taken the time to stack. I continued east and walked for 10 minutes or so and then came to a dirt road. The dirt road looked like it had some wagon tracks in it.

I turned to follow the road north and walked until I came to a T intersection, I stopped and noticed a river and on the other side of the river I saw a wall, there was a path that cut from the river to the wall, it must have been a path cut by people fetching water for their homes, and I assumed that I had come to a walled city. "Aha, people, I thought, now I will be able to find out where I am at."

The wagon trail was cut into a clearing; I'd say that it was about 100 yards across. The trees had been cut back and the stumps dug up and buried or probably even burned. I've heard that some people mill stumps down to use as mulch. I wonder what the case was here. The trees as I looked them over were very large trees. The leaves were very unfamiliar to me. The look and the color of the bark were strange. I knew to be in a place I had never ventured before.

As I walked along the wagon trail, I listened for the sounds of animals and I heard some. I could not tell if the sounds I heard were the songs of mating calls, or warning sounds. I could not isolate any one sound from another. I imagined that to the denizens of this world though it might have been music.

The city was set up against a rocky mountain; the walls were such that they must have been built to withstand the attack of a giant beast. I began the trek down the wagon path to this city; someone surely must be able to tell me where I am at. As I was walking down the path in the distance I saw what was either a carriage or a horse drawn buggy. A small section of the trail had a covered bridge on it that was made out of wood, and was notched to fit together nicely. It was a work of true craftsmanship. The trestles were massive pieces of timber. Laid across the trestles were logs that were cut and notched together so nicely that rain and snow would not come through the cracks.

As I was walking through the bridge, I saw a book lying on the floor, a book which probably fell off of a wagon of some kind, and it showed that not much foot traffic came this way. The book was titled "Ice and Chitin", I paged through it, saw that it was a skill book and put it in my bag.

I continued down the trail and found the main gate to the city. It had an eye built into it for people to walk through. There was a guard on duty; I thought to myself as I approached him, his job was probably to keep vagrants out.

As I got within three feet of the man, "Stop there young man." State your name and your business."

"My name is Eyes in the Mist, and I come from the south looking for work."

"There only be freelance work here mate. There ain't no steady gigs here."

"Where is here anyway?"

"This place be called WINDHELM son."

"If you don't mind, then I'll just see what I can do for myself and most likely be passing on then."

As I passed through the gate, I noticed a small building off to the left, and went in to see if anyone could help me.

I entered the building through a wooden door; again the wood was like no other wood I had seen; the grain and the texture so vastly different. The craftsmanship was extraordinary.

I walked into the building, I saw a shelving unit with many items of various types of material and distinct markings on it. I thought to myself that if I were an archeologist in 100 years and came upon this place, I would probably make mistakes as to what type of people these were. For all I know I am in someone's house.

There was a book lying on the shelf, its title Chronicles Vol. I sounded interesting to me, I looked around; there were about 10 people in the building. I could tell that I was in the first floor of a bar. I hollered out, "Can I buy this book, is it for sale?" No one replied to me, so I picked up the book and put it in my bag. I then left the bar, and headed for wherever my feet took me next.

I walked around the city and found myself coming upon a building that was a Shrine to Talos. It was so familiar to me; it reminded me of the lake front that I had been on not long ago. I thought it strange that I would be able to recognize places and things when I was in a place in which I didn't know where I was.

I entered the building and having no idea what to expect, I did spot a priest off to one side. I pulled the small chest out of my bag and approached the man, and asked him if he would accept this chest for a blessing for me.

I then headed over to a building in the far corner called the New Gnisis Cornerclub. Entering the building I saw that it was a club full of Dark Elves. I walked up to the bartender and asked him for a drink, he drew me a draft and told me that it would be 1 gold coin.

I pulled out the books that I picked up and began to page through them, trying to figure out what they were, as I drank my draft.

The tender approached me and asked, "What are you reading son?"

I then showed him the books.

He told me, "These are skill books; they teach you how to do different things, to make you better and stronger. This land is full of skill books, there are hundreds of them. Save all you can find."

I told him that I would like to buy a round of drinks for the house, and he told me that 10 gold would cover the cost of the drinks and I told everyone that I had bought a round of drinks.

I needed to urinate pretty badly and I also wanted to check the place out, so I asked him where to go and he told me, and I used the opportunity to sneak around a bit, and I found two more books in the basement. An alchemy book called "A Game to Dinner" and I found a book for sneak skill called "The Red Kitchen Reader".

I think that sometimes a title to a book can be quite misleading.

I pocketed both of the books, went back to the bar and grabbed my bag and left.

I asked around about the different types of shops in the area and I was told to check out the White Phial, and there I went. I found the place to be an alchemy establishment. I think that they had everything anyone could ever want. Every type of potion, elixir, and herb could be found there.

I approached the old woman at the counter, and as I got there; she said, "Can I be of some help to you young man?"

"I don't know", I told her.

"Earlier today I found myself in a new place and I was given some gifts and I wonder if you could tell me about them."

I reached into the bag and began setting the vials and bottles on the counter.

"I have no idea what these contain and it seems that I have found someone who might be able to help me."

"Well I shall certainly try to be of some help"

She picked up the bottles one at time and began to inspect the glass and the labels and the contents.

"What is your name young man?"

"I am called Eyes in the Mist. I came to this town looking for clues to where I am and maybe to find some work."

"What kind of work are you looking for, and why do you need to know where you are?"

"I have some skills in a few areas of life, and haven't seen anyone with any signs in their windows, and no one seems to be in any distress of any kind in which I can intervene in their lives and help them." "What about why you are looking for where you are?"

"I found myself to be without memory, and lost this morning."

"Let me tell you something young man, it doesn't matter where you are as long as you live your life to the fullest extent possible."

"I understand what you are saying, but I would still like to know what this means for me."

"We all have trials in life, and you are just facing some right now."

After she went through the bottles, she asked me, "Would you be interested in selling these, or just wanting to know what they are?"

I told her, "I'll sell them to you if your offer sounds good to me. Not knowing what any of them are, you could take advantage of me, and I wouldn't know it. But give me an offer."

She told me, "I'll give you 3, 000 gold for the lot of them, except for the Paralization Potion. "

"It sounds good to me."

I took her offer and left; thankful for the words of encouragement that she gave me.

I found out there was a carriage going to Markarth in the early evening hours. So I went to the town square where the carriage would be and waited.

The carriage arrived without any fanfare of any kind, and the driver jumped down to stretch his legs and the passengers disembarked from the ride. It was a beautiful carriage. The color was gloss black; it looked like it had twenty or more layers of wax. It didn't have a nick at all from what I could see. This owner took care of his business. There was gold piping that lined several areas of the carriage. The interior was a deep, deep red. There were curtains to block the sun. The team of horses was six strong. I could tell by looking at the horses, that fully rested they could easily attain 25 miles per hour and keep it up for a good clip.

I asked the driver how long before we left and he told me that it would be within the hour; he was resting his horses and getting something to eat.

"It'll be 20 gold to get you to Markarth mister."

"Here you go", tossing him the twenty.

I watched as a stable boy came up to the horses and unhitched them and took them away. I reckon that he was going to feed them and brush their coats.

Sure enough within the hour we were on our way.

The carriage stopped at Markarth and let me out and it was off again.

I knew that I needed some more training in sneak. Sneaking around houses and business and the lords and ladies of this land would come in handy. Never know when danger is lurking around the corner. The best way to get training is to do it. So, I took my time in searching every place that I could. I went into the treasury building, the guard tower, the jail. I found the following books: Vernaccus and Bourlor an archery skill book, The Importance of Where a one-handed weapon skill book; there was a book on lock picking called Proper Lock Design, there was a book on alchemy called Herbalists Guide to Skyrim, and there were several others.

After this little bit of adventure, I left downtown Markarth and went to Markarth Ruins. I couldn't get in, so I left the city. I traveled north to a city called Solitude.

Entering the city, I wanted to make my rounds of finding skill books before enlisting the help of a follower. I saw a beggar and gave him a gold piece. I went inside the sleeping area of castle Dour and there were a couple of skill books that I snatched up.

As I was walking around the city and talking to people, there were tales of this ferocious beauty named Illia at a place called the Darklight Tower. I found out that she needed rescuing. If I could rescue her I thought, then I would have a companion to travel with me, to keep me company, to talk to me and to cure the loneliness of living in a strange land. She could teach me the ways of this place, this land and this time. From her I could learn the customs and the language and the manner of dress. Depending on her skill set, I could always use a fellow thief. Maybe she was a warrior with powerful magic. Maybe she was a sorceress. Maybe she was a weapons specialist. I had to find her and ask her for company.

The first stop I had to make was at the Alchemist's Angeline's Aromatic. Angeline Morrard ran the shop with her niece Vivienne Onnis and they lived above the shop. The shop itself was a tiny affair, consisting of a small room with a counter. The walls behind the counter were lined with strange ingredients and dead animals. There were a large number of potions and ingredients to purchase. I needed to buy some poison for my arrows, so that I could easily dispatch of any enemies that would stand in my way of rescuing this woman. The potions that I bought had paralyzing qualities that would work within a couple of seconds.

I continued the search for skill books and found another one at the fletcher called the Golden Ribbon of Merit. There was another skill book in the interior of the castle on Light Armor called the Rear-Guard. There was one more in the Blacksmith's shop sitting inside a crate, I went into sneak and snatched the book out of the crate to later find out that it was a skill book on Light Armor called The Refugees, and yet another in the Bard's College on Alchemy called The Song of the Alchemists, then I moved onto Emperor's Tower and went inside and found a skill book on a table in a small sitting area called Catalogue of Weapon Enchantments. Moving on, Jala's house and there was a symbol on the building just east of the steps and I had no idea of the meaning but I entered the building anyway. There was a pile of Iron Ingots, and upstairs, I found a skill book on Two-Handed called Song of Hrormir. Going back into sneak, I entered the Blue Palace and I roamed around and came to a room where I opened the door and went inside and looking around I saw a shield and I took it, later on, I found out the shield was called the Shield of Solitude. I continued on and came to a place called Northeast Corridor to the left was corridor where a book sat on a low table called Lost Legends the corridor led to a court wizard's bedroom, there were some impressive staff, books and potions about. This room had a small alcove with a skill book and a gem on the bedside cabinet. The skill book was for speech and was called Biography of the Wolf Queen and the gem was the Stone of Barenziah.

I got on a wagon and went off to Riften. I knew the tower was southwest of Riften and needed to get to her quickly. It took no time in finding what I was looking for. After scaling the outer steps, I went inside. Using my bow with all its arrows dipped in paralyzing poison. I set out to find who I looking for. As I entered the first chamber a woman came up to me and told me she needed my help with her mother who was turning into a fiendish hound. She introduced herself to me, and I followed Illia in to all of the areas that she knew and I kept shooting arrows into witches while she slit their throats.

When we reached the top Illia attacked her mother and I shot her with arrows while Illia finished her off. I was able to get over 6200 in gold out of the place plus the Staff of Hag's Wrath. I then asked Illia to go to Bleak Falls Barrow and to wait for me there. I'd be awhile and gave her all of my stuff and said good-bye.

Entering Helgen I found a shop that sold a full set of Imperial Armor: Breastplate, Gauntlets, Boots, Helmet, Greaves, and a Shield, for as low as 380 gold.

Once I had gotten everything that I needed. I was walking around Helgen and I heard that the jail cart was coming and that Ralof was on board and he was to be executed and I knew that I had to rescue him.

So, I waited for the cart to appear, then I told the guard that was escorting the cart from the back that the Jaul in Whiterun needed to talk to him immediately, and that I would take over at the post for him.

After the jailer was gone, I quietly and discreetly got the attention of Ralof and I introduced myself to him as Eye in the Mist a Nord from the North and told him that I was under cover to help and the real ruler of Skyrim to help him escape. Ralof told me that I was either crazy or a spy there to harm the real ruler and I begged him to trust me.

I knew that a dragon was coming and I told him that we needed to wait until then.

Ralof looked at me and asked me how I knew these things. And I told him that I just did. It was an inner sense that I was born with. Then a huge black creature arced through the skies. Landing heavily on Helgen's central tower and unleashed a roar that made everyone both rebel and imperial alike tremble. I watched as this monster scared the holy crap out of everyone and I was laughing up a storm.

After busting Ralof out of jail I told him that we should get down to Riverwood so I can get this show on the road.

For some reason, I knew I had to get to Riverwood trader and tell Lucan that I would get his claw back.

Then I headed out to Bleak Falls Barrow. When I got to the entrance of the Barrow, I saw two dead bandits on the ground and Illia standing over them. I got my stuff back from her, yet I told her to keep all of the gold as she deserved it. Then I went on to tell her about what was in the Barrow and that we needed to work together if this was going to work. I told her that I would love to be her teacher if she wanted to know more than what there is to all magic including Destruction, Restoration, Conjuration, and Alteration and she said she'd be a good student and I told her she wouldn't be a good student, that she'd be a grand student.

Using sneak and going into the Barrow, Illia saw something ahead and then she let loose with a fireball and I with two arrows killing two more bandits. I told her that my arrows would paralyze the target but if she wanted to creep up on the enemy and kill them I would love to watch. She thought that idea was corny.

Next was a puzzle door, which I showed Illia how to operate then we went through.

When we got to the spider chamber, I told Illia to set fire to the place. And within minutes a huge wounded spider fell from the ceiling as did a charred man who was stuck in the web. I went to the man and searched his body and found the Golden Claw.

Then I asked her to summon her three thralls; fire, frost and storm to pave the way for us. She did and they began killing Draugr, also known as Nordic Dead. When we got to the last door, I told Illia that the undead Draugr behind the door was really tough, she would have to use her frost based spells against it while I used my arrows, my flame and sword. Opening the door you could just smell death. It was a ceremonial burial grotto with waterfalls surrounding the long-forgotten chamber. Illia and I separated and I moved to the carved stone center, and onto a word wall. When I was close enough, the word was absorbed within my body and then the creature in the middle of the room rose from its resting place and attacked me not Illia. I shot 9 arrows into its hide and used the sword on it 5 times and hit it with flame 3 times while Illia hit it with her frost spell 3 times before it died.

Before we left, I checked the body and found a stone, that the Draugr was carrying we also looted a chest in the middle of the room and found 573 gold in it.

Back at Riverwood, I gave the claw to Lucan at the Riverwood trader and he gave me 5000 gold. Then I went to Faemdaps house and asked him about the stone that I found, what it was and what I could do with it. I asked him what I could get for the staff that I had, he told me that it was called the Staff of Hag's wrath and he offered me 1310 in gold and I said OK. He told me that I should take the stone to Whiterun and offer it to him.

Between Illia and me we had 16,000 in gold. I knew that I needed some training and decided that I would find some trainers. And I did, and Ralof, Illia and I got some training in lock picking, archery, sneak, pickpocket, speech, illusion, conjuring, destruction, restoration, and enchanting. I asked Faendal if he'd accompany me to Whiterun and he said that he would. I asked Illia if she too would come along and she said that she would.

We fast traveled to Whiterun and I found that Jarl Balgruuf the Greater was leader of Whiterun. I went in search of a guard and asked to talk to Jarl and when the guard asked why, I told him that Helgen was just attacked by dragons and he should send his army for protection. When I finally got to see Jarl, I told him about the attack on Helgen and that I needed to see his wizard Farengar. When his wizard came forward I pulled out the stone and handed it to him. His eyes got wide as he reached out for the stone saying he's never... Before he could finish, I also told him about the word wall and that my body absorbed the writings and I showed him. Touching the symbols with his hand he murmured that the legend must be true as it has already begun with the return of the dragons. He then called for an errand boy or something, said something to him and the boy ran out.

As I finished my conversation about the Dragonstone a guard rushed in yelling a dragon has been sighted nearby. I told him that I would take care of this, just make sure your archers can hit what they aim at. Taking off, we ran through the castle explaining what must be done. A guard yells for Irileth who is the captain and tells her to meet us at the Chillfurrow Farm and bring his archers. At the same time, Illia, Faendal and I are getting into position for the big battle. When the creature started to circle overhead, everyone got into position and began to assault the dragon. Ralof, I called to him, watch my back. He came running over and with his blade out he began to watch my back. Then the attack started and everything was shot at the dragon. Arrows, fire, frost, and more arrows, fire and frost until the dragon fell to the ground. Afterwards, I approached the dead dragon. As I got close it began to bum, the crackling flesh merged into the ethereal soul of the dragon and while everyone watched, the maelstrom of energy and light began to swirl around me and my body actively absorbed the soul of the dragon.

Returning to Dragonreach, I told Jarl that I could absorb the soul of a dragon, my reward was a trek to meet the greybeards. I was also named Thane of Whiterun with another follower named Lydia. I wanted to meet her and she what kind of person she really was.

She was a housecarl which is a person who would follow you and may even be a marriage prospect . I really did want the house because I needed a place for all of us, and especially a safe place to put all the skill books that I was collecting. But I did accept the title, and I wanted to meet these beards, so we started our trek. Once there, the beards wanted to know so much but I could only tell them so little. They however, had me approach two of their word walls and watched as my body absorbed the words. Then I had to learn how to use them as I absorbed the dragon souls. Speech skill would help a great deal when using a power word. I, with my followers, all five of us left for

Whiterun. Arriving in Whiterun, I stopped off at the Drunken Huntsman to check out the skill book, on Archery it was called The Black Arrow Volume 2 and stole it. My next stop was the Bannered Mare. I gave everyone 200 gold each and asked them to go all over town and buy up as many skill books as they could carry, and bring them back to Breezehome, and set them in different stack so that I can tell the books apart. I also told everyone to wait for me there.

I went to Dragon Bridge in Haalfinger and talked Horgir about a favor. I had to get his axe and chop 1000 pieces of wood for 5 gold each. I traveled to eleven other people in eleven more areas chopping wood for them for a total of 60,000 gold. I then went to 9 other areas and mined ore for 9 people and earned gold for my work. By the time I was done, I had made 327, 000 gold.

Then I headed back to Whiterun, at Breezehome and asked my friends if they wanted to go to the Smuggler's Den and that we should go raid it, as we needed more experience than what we would get for just raiding towns. I told them that the chest was trapped and if you try to open it, the rest of the gang would return and ambush us. So we killed two guards and then waited for the rest of the gang to return and we ambushed them. We finally opened the chest and found 560 gold.

Our next big break came at Fellglow Keep where I asked everyone to be forever watchful, if you see something you want to touch, ask me first. I had asked Ralof to bring up the rear whenever we go in a straight line and watch our backs. I asked Faendal to use his bow and be forever watchful and gave him some poison to dip his arrows in and gave poison to the other members of the party to put on their weapons as well. Then came Illia, I told her to be careful and that I won't know what I'd do if she got killed and she gave me a little smirk and I took the lead in sneak and when I thought it was safe, I'd motion for the others to keep low and follow. When we got to a safe point, I motioned Ralof to check out an area. He motioned for me to join him to pick a couple of locks and to set off some traps. Moving on we came to a room where a mage was training some students and had Illia summon a flame thrall to kick some butt. I guess the heat got to be too much for them. The thrall continued on through the ruins. I had Illia summon three more thralls to go through the whole complex and kill everything that stood in their way, and then wait for further instructions. Then I went through the whole place unlocking chests and everyone else went through behind me collecting gold and loot. At the end of the day, I took 1,000 gold for myself and let everyone else have more than me. The final door inside the ruins was locked and only I could walk through the door while everyone else was forced to wait outside. My bow was ready and my fingers were already starting to get tired then I saw her approach from the dark and I lowered my bow a bit but didn't ease the tension of the bowstring. Then I fired hitting her in the leg. Fool, you will die! She screamed at me. She was pissed and then she summoned Atronachs to deal with me but they didn't stick around long as she was losing her power and her life then she keeled over and died. I grabbed the three skill books that were there and left.

I asked Illia to go to the College of Winterhold and wait for me; that I would be there in a week. I then returned to Whiterun and went to Jorrvaskr and asked to speak with Aela about joining her ranks. I had to leave Ralof and Faendal behind as I was in pursuit of another passion. I chose to join the Companions! My first assignment was to go to the Pelagia farm and give a hand with a giant. Arriving there I saw three people trying to take down a giant that was wielding a huge club. I pulled my bow and shot it three times, hitting the giant: once in the leg, once in the stomach, and once in the neck. Five seconds later he was going down. When it was over, they said good work and that anything that was on the giant was mine to take. They told me to meet them back at the Jorrvaskr in Whiterun if I was worth anything in a fight.

Entering the hall, I was met by Skjor and Farkas and told me that I was going with them as we went for a trek through the wilderness to Dustman's Cairn. Inside I armed myself and began to navigate through the catacombs and listened to Farkas' advice. I was told to take any treasure I descended past. When I could go no further a cage dropped over me separating me from Farkas who was surrounded by the members of the silver hand and I couldn't get out to help him. Then he backed up against the cage let out a guttural growl and transformed into a massive werewolf and slaughtered the silver hand where they cowered. Then he changed back to his human form. After freeing me, he asked me what I thought and I said it was great. Upon nearing a word wall, the words were absorbed by my body. And there was a fragment of Ysgramor's Blade on a and pedestal which I took. Then returning to Jorrvaskr I met with the other Blades of Companionship and I spoke to Aela and she took me outside and in the back of the building. Then I was given a drink and then I was to gaze upon a massive segment of magic and told to hang on.

Later on, I woke up on the moor clad in little more than my modesty. Aela the Huntress was with me and explained that my transformation was not easy but successful. Dressing, Aela told me of a Silver Hand clan nearby and we were going to kill them all. Once inside I mentioned to Aela the we could just paralyze them, and then let the others just eat them alive but a quick death would be better. Many of my brethren lay dead in the cells but the ones that were still living. Before we left, we re-gathered the fragments of Wuuthred and then looted the place and headed back to Whiterun. While we were gone, several Silver Hands came into town and killed three of our clan members. Kodiak was among them. Now, it was revenge.

Going down to the underground we grieved for a lost comrade. I passed another word wall of animal allegiance before I left for the rift to pick up an amulet of Mara and asked Aela to accompany me to Riften. When we got there, I asked her to wait for me at Bolli's house while I went to get the amulet before returning to her.

When I walked into the house and Aela saw me then she saw the Amulet and knew right away why I had brought her here. We both went to the temple and were married. Now, I had a follower and a companion. Whatever we did as one now we did together, we then became one.

Going to Solitude we managed to infiltrate Northwatch Keep and after sneaking all the way through and removing all the traps, we pretty much slaughtered everyone inside then collected two skill books called: Orsinium which was for Heavy Armor, Catalogue of Armor Enchantments for enchanting, and Words and Philosophy which was a book on two-handed weapons. There were also 3 chests worth 560 gold pieces.

The next place that we went to was Rimerock Burrow where we snuck through removing all the traps and killing everyone and taking their gold which totaled 1062. Our next target was Volskugge. We entered, disarmed all the traps then went into Beast Mode and killed thirty one in all and fed on four of them. When it was all over, we came away with a Dragon Priest Mask (Volsung) 6540 gold pieces, and more experience.

Our next objective was Lost Echo Cave which had one skill book Surfeit of Thieves on lock picking.

Then we went to Wolfskull cave/ruins. We had to make sure that both of us were very healthy before entering this cave. I used my sneak along with my bow and took down five necromancers and one Draugr, and I got another skill book called Racial Phylogeny which was for Restoration magic, we also found 36 potion bottles and 40 scrolls, from the cave. I thought that I would keep the scrolls for Illia.

Then we decided to go to Winterhold to meet up with Illia. Once we got there we entered the College and looked around for a Wizard named Faralda who was a trainer in destruction. When we found him, I told Illia to get 10 training lessons from him.

We went to Hela's folly, where I shot an Argonian and took his gemstones and rubies.

Aela approached me as we were traveling back towards Winterhold and suggested that I incorporate Illia into the companions and I told her that it wouldn't work out as she and I were already companions and Illia would only try to ruin it for us, and when she understood what I meant, she thought it was a bad idea. I asked her what she thought about moving to Markath. She told me she saw the place and she liked it, but in order to own the house I would have to become Thane of the Reach. I would have to remember that on my way back this way. Meanwhile, my companion and Illia and I were heading for Bthardamz to collect some Dwarven relics and sell them to a fence because I knew they would fetch a good price. But Aela wanted to go to Whiterun to see if there were any more quests for her to do. I asked her to go there and wait for me, and that I would be along later. So I went to Belethor at his General Goods Store in Whiterun. While there, I wanted to check on (spread) a rumor that the Silver Hands were tied in with the Silver- Blood and were the ones that orchestrated the attack on Jorrvaskr and killed the people inside. Then while at the General store I was able to pick up the skill book Speech: Biography of the Wolf Queen.

Then I also told Belethor that someone should inform Farkas that a spy was staying at the Bannered Mare.

I then went to Arcadia's Cauldron to buy some fast acting poison for my arrows and blade. Which I was able to pick up a Restoration skill book called Withershins. The potions cost me 300 gold. Then I went to Warmaiden's to buy a Composite Longbow and 60 more arrows. Thirty for me and thirty for Illia and gave her my old bow. Here, I told her a present for you. Unbeknownst to us Aela had been doing what came naturally to her. When Illia and I went to see her at the Jorrvaskr, she wasn't there, apparently she and 6 of her companions ran out of there in a great hurry, Hmm, I wondered if my talk with Belethor had anything to do with it. We waited around for a while then Illia and I headed over to Riverwood but not before telling someone at Jorrvaskr where we had gone so that they could tell Aela.

After hooking back up with Ralof, he asked me to talk to Arngeir. Arngeir asked me to go to Ustengrav and find the Horn of Jurgen Windcaller, and to return with it, anything else was mine to keep. I asked Arngeir where Ustengrav was and he told me it was Cragwallow Slope. Illia and I travelled there.

When we got there I asked Illia to summon three flame thralls to help us deal with the necromancer, while I dealt with the bandits. Then descending into the abyss in sneak mode, I asked Illia to use her most dangerous and destructive spell. Illia had all kinds of creatures running around the place, scaring the people inside and setting off traps and killing the bad people. When it was over, I found the Horn of Jurgen an alteration skill book The Lunar Lorkhan. Looked in several chests and took out about 3000 gold. Heading back to the High Hrothgar and heading through the monastery until I spotted Arngeir I handed him the horn and he remembered that the time had come for the Greybeards to recognize me as Dragonborn.

I stepped up onto the glowing runes and as everyone watched including Illia; my body absorbed the word of power as Arngeir spoke the word Dah. Everyone stood at a diamond stance as I withstood the blast of power with each interval. Heading back to Riverwood, I went to see Delphine in the Sleeping Giant Inn and asked her what was up. She told me of a pattern that involved me and Dragons. The next Dragon would be rising from the dead, and she needed to stop it. We had to travel to Jynesgrove in Eastmarch. So, fast traveling to Windhelm, we turned southeast towards Narzulbur.

Aldvin was there hovering overhead, resurrecting his brethren then flew off. The skeletal Sahloknir climbed out of his grave and was resurrected by Aldvin's powerful magic. Before Sahloknir's skin could gather around his bones and he regained his powers. I raced in with my most impressive melee implement and delivered a series of attack arrows to weaken the dragon's health. Delphine fired arrows, then rushed in with attacks when the dragon landed; when Sahloknir had been reduced back into a pile of bones, the beast split apart into hundreds of scaly shards. I then absorbed another dragon soul. I then searched the dragon, and then went over to Delphine for her promised revelations. Our next move was to find out who was controlling these dragons, and the Thalmor. I needed some training in Destruction and the three masters were in Windhelm, Solitude and Winterhold so it was off to Windhelm first.

Our next stop, Markarth. Entering the main gate, it looked like a massacre had taken place. Everyone we saw was dead and we went checking bodies. We came away with 3, 600 gold pieces but no companions. We checked a little bit more into town and then left. We went up to the mine and looked in. We couldn't hear a sound so we went inside. Everyone was dead. I had Illia stand guard while I explored. I was able to get in and get out and we were just standing around yelling when a contingent of soldiers came marching by.

We left and went to see the Raerek Steward to see about helping out. He asked if I could get rid of all of the dead bodies and clean up the street. I said sure. It took almost 5 hours but it was clean when he came through for an inspection. When he asked what I wanted as a reward, I told him that I wanted to buy the Vlindrel Hall. He thought for a moment and said he'd give it to me if I'd become Thane of the Reach. I thought about it for a moment and said yes.

We met Argis the Bulwark at the house and offered him one of the bedrooms to sleep in as I was after all the Thane. When I asked what happened, I was told that a pack of werewolves came in at night and killed every single Silver-Blood that lived, it was a massacre. Then what happened, I asked. Then they left. I asked Illia to stay there as I was going to look for Aela.

I went as far back as Whiterun and waited for Aela to show up but I waited and waited. Where could she be? I began checking out the underforge and found her nearly dead from something. She needed to feed so I offered her some of me. When she turned into beast form and sunk her teeth into me, I could almost feel the power she was drawing from me.

I didn't realize it at the time, but later it dawned on me that I offered her the power of the Dragonborn that flowed through my blood. It took her about three days to recover fully.

Then I took her to the reach and showed her that she had her own house. My quest not yet over. We would make the companions stronger; she would go where I went. Leading her, she would follow me and also guide Illia to use her spells and summon a mighty storm thrall or two to clear our path.

We assigned Njada and Ria to attract new members with the Companions both males and females, as many as were needed. Aela and I went off to continue our adventure. Our loyalties lay with the Stormcloaks, the Thieves Guild and the Dark Brotherhood, and especially the companions.

I was not yet up to my full potential as Aela was as I still had training to undergo. I had asked Aela if I could go off on my own for a few months and train and she told me that she would pray for me. We hugged and kissed and said our so-longs. My first stop was the College of Winterhold, I found someone to give me twenty lessons that I needed so that I could train in Illusion.

My next stop was in Riften where I did odd jobs for members of the Guild. I had to strike up a deal with Majhad, a Khajiit to give him half of everything I brought in if he trained me up to level fifty on pickpocket and they both agreed to 3,000 gold pieces. My first job was to pilfer a ring from Madesi's stall and place it in the pocket of on Brandi-Shei. To do this, I also had to get training in Sneak from Delvin Mallory for a special chore that he would send me on when the time was right.

Afterwards, I was given 100 gold but kept it for my bosses. My next job was to collect 100 gold each from three different shopkeepers. For this, I received one poison, one healing potion and one fortify skill potion, and 150 gold. My next job was to go to the Goldenglow Estate break in and steal Queen Bee Statue, Goldenglow bill of sale and set blaze to four of the hives. The estate was west of Riften. I immediately thought of Illia and as I went out to do the job, I returned to the house and Markarth and picked up Illia and together we traveled to the island shore just northwest of the estate. I told Illia to cast fire across the lake to and on the beehives there when she saw my signal. I then swam up to the property and entered through the sewer. With bow drawn, I snuck in and retrieved everything I was told to get including 3,000 gold. Afterwards I met Illia across the lake and I asked her to stick around that I might need her services again. Back at the guild, I met up with Mercer Frey and handed him the key to the safe, the key to the cellar, the Queen Bee statue and the bill of sale and I told him that I had set three hives on fire and the fourth began by itself as the people tried to put out the fire. I got 400 gold pieces for that job. My next job was a simple one, go in and poison the grain and ale then leave, no problem. I was gone three days on this one and I told the boss that I did three trial runs before I thought that I was ready. I turned over the Honning Brew Meadery Key and 500 gold, getting 2000 gold for the job.

Next I was go to Solitude and find an Argonian named Gulum-Ei, I sent Illia ahead to prepare for my arrival. I was drawn to Winking Skeever Tavern as I saw Illia waiting outside. Going inside, I looked around the room checking things out. Spotting the Argonian, I approached his table and sat down next to him. We talked and talked then he left.

I told Illia that she needed to go to the Blue Palace and steal a case of Firebrand Wine from Eilisit's room without getting caught and return here with it and she was off. I on the other hand shadowed Gulum-Ei. Stopping at the East Empire Shipping Office, I picked up a map. Going into the Warehouse I climbed to higher ground and got into it and looted the place. Returning to the Inn, I asked Illia to bring the wine with her that we were going to Riften. Once we were back at the Cistern, I went on ahead and revealed my information to Mercer Frey. Mercer's demeanor changed when I handed him the bill of sale for the Goldenglow Estate and mentioned Karliah's name. Mercer told me he knew where she was and asked me to kill her for him. He told me that she was at Snow Veil Sanctum. Before I was to leave, I was offered some new armor as a reward. I looked around for Illia who much to my surprise was talking with Gulum-Ei who was holding the case of wine. I asked her if she would follow me and watch my back. But I wanted her to return to Whiterun, go to Jorrvaskr and tell Aela to meet me at the Snow Veil Sanctum as it's the Last of the Silver-Hand and that is where I'd be. I then travelled there with Mercer Frey and asked him to trust me and to trust in whatever he sees that no harm will come to him. I told Mercer that we have a campaign coming. She is going to wait for you here while I go and disarm any traps inside then we are going to have you follow us inside and we are going to find Karliah for and disarm her then he can kill her as this is only for him. Then when Aela arrived I told her what was happening and then we entered the ruins. I went in to disarm all the traps and when I returned to Mercer and Aela, Aela and I told Mercer to just follow us. Then Aela changed shape and went off running, then I changed into my new armor and followed her. Then after a while, I arrived at a gate and then my vision blurred and I blacked out. When I came to, I saw a woman standing over me. She explained that aside from saving my life and the life of my companion who lay half naked beside me. She was asking for my help in tracking Mercer down. I told her I didn't know, that I would have to check with my wife first.

After talking with Aela, she agreed to the terms and apologized for believing she was a Silver-Hand. Karliah handed me a journal and asked me to take it to Winterhold and find Enthir, a good friend of Gallus, who may be able to decipher it.

Arriving in town, I began going to each building asking for Enthir. When I got to the frozen Hearth, he held up his hand and said he was there. After looking over the journal, he told me that the text was very old and that I had to go to Markarth and talk with the court wizard. And then asking him to review the journal wasn't too hard for a favor later on.

Later on, back at Ratwau, Karliah and Aela were waiting for me. Opening the gate, all the guild members were waiting for us and asked why we were with a murderer and I showed them the journal and they let us in.

Brynjolf couldn't believe Mercer had been stealing from the guild so he ordered Delvin to open the vault. It was empty, everything was gone. We must find this man and get revenge I spouted. Yes, Vex chimed in; I vow to kill Mercer immediately. Brynjolf ordered everyone to guard the Ragged Flagon. Then he turned to me, Karliah, and Aela and asked what we learned. After I told him, he asked us to break into Mercer's house in Riften known as Rifitweald Manor and find out where he has gone. My first quest from here was to find a quill in the lake under a small island inside a sunken row boat.

Once I had the quill, I continued onto Mercer's house. I had asked Aela and Karliah to have their bows ready with their paralyzing arrows and watch my back and their own as well. A side gate was open and a key was lying on top of a stump with a note that read "key to Mercer's house". Taking out my bow, I aimed it a mechanism and fire it and it brought down a ramp. Then we had a much more stealthy way into the residence. We climbed down the ramp and used the house key to unlock the door. Any bandits we came across while sneaking were shot and slaughtered. Downstairs we found a trap door that led to the basement where Mercer left his gold and plans. We also found a sword called Chillrend and a bust of the gray fox. Back at Ragged Flagon, we gave Brynjolf the plans. He then turned to Karliah and asked her if we all could meet at the Great Standing Stone and go from there. Karliah agreed and we all met at the Great Standing Stone where Karliah pressed a spot on the cliff and a door opened. Stepping through the still air of the entrance tunnel, we followed Karliah, Brynjolf, Aela and myself to the armory to don the Armor of a Nightingale and begin the oath.

Our roles then became increasingly clearer. Now we had to head to Irkngthand in the mountains above Lake Yorgrim but not before we picked up our other gear. But first, we needed the rest of our Brethren. Karliah was to retrieve the thieves (all if necessary) and Aela was to retrieve the Companions (saying that one Last Silver Hand remained) but made everyone swear on their lives that this was to be kept a secret. Aela returned with twelve Companions and Karliah returned with nine thieves making it twenty-five warriors. We all met at Irkngthand. Outside stood a complement of bandits who the Companions all slaughtered and feasted upon. We then headed west under the fallen columns and up onto the upper ledge next to the Dwarven exterior, and on southeast. Halting the party, I went into sneak and went on ahead disarming all the traps, a few minutes later I returned and told everyone that the coast was clear except for bandits. We found the rickety wooden steps and followed the precarious path across the domed rooftops and over the wooden bridges to the upper entrance at the main structure, Irkngthand Arcanex. Then stepping into the golden gloom, bodies were everywhere with deep gashes and/ or teeth marks in them. Moving along we came to an elevator that took us all down to the Grand Cavern. At the bottom, we had to pull two levers, one first then run across the way and pull the other lever on the opposite ledge. Each lever lights a lamp by the door and each lamp has to be lit in order to get through the door so only one had to stay behind. Once through the door, I saw several scrolls that I thought may come in handy so I grabbed up a few, (8) to be exact.

At the entrance, my route opened up into a massive grand cavern. Seeing Mercer below I quickly fired an arrow and just as he cast a spell several companions jumped on him and began tearing him apart. After they were done, I searched his body and found Right Edge of the Falmer and the Skeleton Key. We then retraced our steps opening up all the chests and we found the left of the Falmer, as well as 7, 566 gold pieces, and finally back outside.

Brynjolf said he had matters to attend to and took off. Then Karliah approached me with a token of her esteem, A Nightingale Bow, now it was my turn to travel the Pilgrim's Path and return the Skeleton Key in the Twilight Sepulcher. After I returned the key, I was rewarded with "The Agent of Strife" a power that I could cast once a day that takes 100 points of health damage from a target and gives it to me. Then I see a flash of light and I'm back outside the Sanctuary. Karliah was there and explained that whenever I wanted, I could come to visit as Nightingale was her home. I told Aela that looked real pretty in black and hoped that she would always wear it at home meaning all of Markarth.

Moving on we had a few jobs to do yet. After I was done, I was made leader of the Thieves Guild wardrobe. I told them to meet me at Vlindrel Hall and I'd meet them there in a few days. I said my fare-wells to the party and I was off to join the Brotherhood.

Oh what a life this web we weave for ourselves. I had to go to the road just north of Whiterun and advise a farmer to help out a man with a wagon.

Afterwards, I was to find a boy who ran off from an orphanage by asking about rumors at the Sleeping Giant Inn in Riverwood. And then on to Candlehearth Hall in Windhelm when finally the name Aventus Aretino came up. Then going to the Honorhall Orphanage in Riften, I entered the premises and watched as Grelod the Kind didn't live up to her name. Once Grelod had ordered the children to bed, I left the building and went to Windhelm where I found Aventus at his family's house. When I entered the building I heard Aventus reciting the Black Sacrament. After listening to what that child had told me, I was more than angered. I told the child that justice would prevail. I returned to the Orphanage and waited until night time and snuck inside and placed a lightning rune and a fire rune at the head of the bed where Grelod was sleeping, and then I left and waited at the Scorched Hammer for sun-up and the explosion that came with the dawn of the sun.

When nothing happened I went to knock at the door and I had to knock loud and it happened, a really big BOOM. I about ripped the door off the hinges just trying to get inside. Yup, the old crone was burned to death. And no one was the wiser. Back at Aventus Aretino's home he paid me with his family heirloom. So I thought I needed a rest so I went back to Markarth and went to sleep in my house. The next thing I knew Aela is waking me up saying someone was there to talk to me. I sat up in bed and listened to her. But I wasn't home, I was inside some shack and I had to converse with a mysterious veiled figure in black. She introduced herself as Astrid, representative of the Dark Brotherhood.

Although I have demonstrated an aptitude for deathcraft and would be an asset to the Brotherhood, I have created a problem. I began to ask if I could talk now, and permission was given. I told Astrid that by knowing that she was the leader of such an organization, I would be honored to follow in her footsteps in becoming part of the organization of the Dark Brotherhood. With such as she had there, I simply slit the throat of the Khajiit and told her that he was her spy. He replied, how did you know why you were here? I told her that I knew a lot of things and that my next quest was to meet the Brotherhood. I followed Astrid back to the Sanctuary and met the family. First assignment, go to Markarth and seek out Muiri, who may be hanging around inside the Silver Blood Inn.

Yes, I interrupted and said I know about Alain Dufont and left. When I arrived in Markarth, I sent word to Aela and asked for her help. I contacted Muiri and told her that I would be happy to avenge her broken heart but first I needed to know where the evil man was. Before I left, Muiri offered me some Lotus Extract. Aela and I headed for Raldbthar. As we approached we were met by bandits and I let loose with a flame thrall, a frost thrall, and a storm thrall who killed all the bandits. Then we entered the complex and descended the stairs. The thralls went first and yet Aela and I readied our bows. Then when I was sure it was him, I fired an arrow and the thralls went in for the kill.

We picked up a unique weapon, Aegisbane and also Alain and hauled his butt back to Muiri for safe keeping under lock and key. We also gave Muiri her ring back. Then it was off to see Nilsine Shatter- Shield in Windhelm. We were going under false pretenses in order to get close to Nilsine and the other members of the house before kidnapping Nilsine and taking her back to Muiri to be put into Cidhna Mine Holding Cell where they will die, slowly. Then when (1) reported back to Astrid and introduced Aela to her and asked to find some work for her. My next job was to travel to the earthen mound of Volunruud northeast from there. Once I was at the mound, I had a small altercation with the Draugr warriors. I met with a man named Amaund Motierre who gave me a jeweled amulet and a sealed letter I was to give to Astrid and I did.

My next assignment was to kill Vittoria Vici in Solitude. First I wanted to go to her house, which to my surprise was unlocked. The main floor of the house was comprised of a hallway, living area and a kitchen there were books to read and there was food to eat. Upstairs was a balcony library and a bedroom with a chest. In the cellar was an exit and a display case with what looked like a valuable weapon. I snatched up all that I could. Then in going there, I waited for her to return and start her speech then I pushed the statue off onto her head. Then it was back to Astrid.

My next job was to kill Gaius Maro and plant an incriminating letter on his body. I went to the covered bridge. Waited until he went for a walk then approached him stabbed him and stuck the letter in his pocket.

I reported back to Gabriella. My next job was to find any evidence in Cicero's chamber. I found a journal and gave it to Astrid. Astrid wanted me to go to the Dawnstar Sanctuary as quickly as possible and have secured a steed named Shadow-mere. Fast traveling to Dawnstar, I headed down the stairs and I could hear Cicero deeper in the maze say that Astrid has sent the best to defeat me. In sneak I stepped on a plate but the trap didn't go off.

Then, on a snow bridge, I spotted an Udefrykte and used the word "Roan" meaning animal allegiance which made the Udefrykte friendly and let me pass. Then I said "Mir" which meant allegiance, then as I entered the sanctuary the Udefrykte rushed in to attack the Sanctuary Guardians then as I spied Cicero lying flanked by two skeletons, I readied my bow with the paralyzing poison on the arrow and fired hitting Cicero in the torso. I waited until he was unconscious then I looted his body and left four fire runes and four lightning runes next to him doing a total of 400 points of damage, then I left 6 more of each next to the entrance of the sanctuary just in case.

Back at the Brotherhood Sanctuary I told Astrid that Cicero was dead.

My next job was to kill Anton Virane. I got into his baking shop and placed four each of fire, frost and lightning runes around his shop where he did all his cooking. Need I say more? I was able to get the Gourmet's Writ of Passage to Festus Krex. My next job was to assassinate the Emperor.

Astrid told me that I had to go to the Castle Dour in Solitude and present the Gourmet's Writ of Passage to the officer in charge who was Commander Maro. She also told me that I was to prepare a special meal for the Emperor with an extra ingredient that she handed to me. This had to take some thinking. I traveled to Solitude but I stopped by Angeline's Aromatic's for some special ingredients of my own; Blue Mountain Flower and Wheat which caused the person to become sleepy or it could kill the victim. I found Commander Maro and showed him the Gourmet's Writ of Passage.

In the kitchen Gianna was busy preparing the banquet feast. I explained to her that I was the Gourmet and wanted to show her how to make a broth that would lift the Emperor's spirits and pulled out the Blue Mountain flower and wheat and added it to the broth. The Emperor just loved it and felt really good afterwards.

Later, I told Gianna that the next time she served broth to put in the Blue Mountain flower; I gave her something that really wasn't Blue Mountain flower. I left for the sanctuary. When I got there, Commander Maro's men were ransacking the place. I pulled my bow and began dropping his men. I killed everyone that I could, then it ended, but how could this have happened? A voice behind me confessing to have betrayed the Brotherhood, now her life must end and I had to rebuild the Brotherhood and take Astrid's sword and run her through with it. No one betrays the Brotherhood and lives. Only Nazir and Babette remained, as I came to grips with my family's slaughter.

I told Babette and Nazir that the Night Mother had spoken to me and we had to rebuild at the Dawnstar Sanctuary. I put Nazir in charge of recruiting new members while I continued on with what must be done. I headed to Solitude and heard that the Emperor was on his boat. So I headed for the docks, and met the Commander there and killed him. Next, I got on board and began to sneak around taking out any sailors that got in my way. There must have been thirty of them, all of them in my way, and they fell just as they came to me; until it was only the Emperor and I remaining.

I was able to kill the Emperor; then I ransacked his quarters for anything of value. I was able to find gold which I took to Dawnstar Sanctuary. I then took Shadow-mere and continued to fulfill the contracts and became the leader of the Dark Brotherhood.

My next quest was to finish off the Dragonborn assignments. There was Aela in Markarth & Illia at the house and others waiting for me to return. I decided to return home to a loving wife and a nice warm and cozy bed. The next day Aela and I headed out with Illia. Our first adventure was to go to the Stone Quarter of Windhelm.

Apparently, we were to check out the strange lights that onlookers were seeing inside the Hierjim House. Aela and I arrived in Windhelm that evening and met with Tova Shattershield who for one gave us a key to the old manor. The next day Aela and I entered the house around 3:00 in the afternoon and noticed that the house had been cleared out, cobwebs were everywhere. The place was deserted, but a thorough inspection revealed the following: the front room contained a chest that had blood spatter on it, and was recently pushed against the wall. I suggested to Aela that we may need a Storm of Frost Thrall to aid us in our search and let them just linger about while Aela and I continued searching.

Searching the chest, I found almost a dozen leaflets warning of a 'butcher' named Viola Giordano. There was also a journal which made for some grisly reading. There was also a wardrobe cabinet at the back of the room that was nailed to the wall. Opening it and searching it I found a false panel which revealed a small makeshift altar and antechamber with body parts about.

Another journal was found along with an amulet behind the Altar.

Leaving the house and having the thralls stay there as not to scare the crap out of the townsfolk, we consulted with a guard. It was at that moment that we heard a crash which came from inside the house. Just as we re-entered the house, one of the thrall's was chasing a woman upstairs while the other thrall was going through a secret door in the west wall. Aela followed the woman and I followed through the secret door. Apparently when I reached the basement I had to do battle with a man & a woman but then Aela came through a secret door apparently from upstairs and got the man with one of her arrows. I on the other hand got the woman with the Sword of Woe. The guard that was with us saw everything. The man confessed to everything and he was taken away. I took the amulet back to the College of Winterhold and asked the Master-Wizard there to lock it up. Then I returned to Windhelm with Aela.

Our next quest was to find a lost legend and it began at Reachwater Rock east of Markarth, north of Reachwind Eyrie and west of Old Hroldan. Well, it wasn't that hard to find, or locate. We had to make sure we were ready for this one. I looked at Aela and asked her if she was ready and she said she was and then asked me if I was ready. I told her that I was and she said let's go then. Then I said to her, Wait, I love you and then we left. I guess it took a moment or two for what I said to sink in. She fell behind a little bit. We looked for Reachwater Rock and got a little wet entering the cavern. A dead adventurer lay against a tree and a pedestal stood nearby. There were two items of interest on the pedestal, an ancient edict and an Emerald Dragon Claw.

I quickly snatched up the claw, and then checked the dead body. He had a book called "Lost Legends of Skyrim", three healing potions. A Nordic puzzle wall was behind the pedestal. According to the book, we had to go to Fogunthur just southeast of Solitude. So we traveled to Fogunthur. Using the Emerald Dragon Claw, we opened the gate. There on another Pedestal was an Ivory Dragon Claw which we used to open the next gate where a piece of Gauldur's Amulet lay next to Gauldur's Blackblade and a writ of sealing. When we got the Writ, Lord Griemund's Key and Epitaph appeared. We moved on to yet another pedestal that had another piece of Gauldur's Amulet, Gauldur's Blackbow and a Writ of Sealing. Then another pedestal appeared with the Staff of Jyrik Gauldurson, Gauldur Amulet piece and writ of Sealing. Then we got to a word wall and my body absorbed the Power Word: Ice form. Then it was back to Reachwater Rock where we entered the Hall. We continued down the steps beyond and entered the Archmage Gauldur's tomb. We approached the altar at the far (northwest) end of the elaborately constructed room where there were three amulet pedestals. Then three spectral forms appeared and set us a challenge. Defeat us or die, what say you. They attacked with the upmost force but I defeated them. After I delivered the final blow to Jyrik, the three spectral brothers regrouped at the Altar.

Suddenly, the Sarcophagus behind them opened. The brothers turned, Sigdis let out a shout and a brilliant blast of light wiped them from existence. When the dust settled, a spectral figure appeared and granted me what I sought: In a flash of light, the Amulet fragments combined. Also in the sarcophagus and on Gauldur's skeleton, we found 67, 615 gold. Stopping off at the Sanctuary, I donated 10,000 gold to the new Dark Brotherhood. Then I gave Aela all my things and had her hold onto them while I checked out the Cidhna mine. I went in to check out the Markarth Ruins with the key just in case something happened to me but I came out safely.

Our last adventure was to retrieve or secure the attunement sphere from Septimus Signus. It all began by going out to Septimus Signus's Outpost straight north from the College of Winterhold. Then, after we had the sphere, we had to go to the Blackreach Elevator in the Pale. First, I needed to stock up on poison arrows as did Aela we also asked Illia if she wanted to do one last adventure and she agreed.

After refitting everyone in the new armor, we went down to the elevator in Blackreach. We needed to get rid of all the Falmer. In sneak everyone crept along gathering up Crimson Nirnroot as we went. We had our bows out and Illia wanted to summon a few helpers. Moving on to our first stop, Sinderion's field laboratory where we found a workbench and a skill book. We made our way to a shrine picking up Crimson Nirnroot as we went. It would be dark soon and we needed to a safe place to look out from. We then moved to the guard towers. We needed to explore more and I wanted to get near the Gong of Vulthuryol and I had a plan. Sneaking over by the pumping station and used, fus do unslaad rahgol ahrkyulom and the dragon came flying out of its nest and set fire to everything before landing on the south road. I approached the south road and waited for the dragon to land.

Then I said "Roan mir" which meant animal allegiance. Vulthuryol looked at me and I began to explain who I was as if its thoughts were in my head and I could hear it talking to me. I thought you could help us, my wife and friend to defeat the Falmer and I will set you free in the upper world. It agreed and I went running back to Aela and Illia and told them to get to cover and we all ran to an elevator and closed the door and locked it. We waited and listened and waited. There were lots of explosions and lots of yelling and screaming then it was all quiet. We quickly opened the doors but didn't see the dragon anywhere. I told the others to find the dragon and I would come and help.

It was lying over by the fungus field. I swiftly began to heal it as it slept. We took turns watching and guarding that great beast. The next morning we all searched the elevators for the easiest way up and found one that would bring him out at Alftand. I told him to visit the throat of the world. Then we said our good-byes and told him to come visit me in Markarth. Then we went back to collecting our Nirnroot and loot.

Our next quest and last was to go to the Hall of the Vigilant in the Pale so we went there. Arriving we were to begin a main quest, a new quest as Vampire Hunters. We accepted the blessing at the Altar but the proprietor said we were still diseased and we told him that we preferred it that way because of the Vampires; he told us that we'd have to deal with it then.

Then taking us out back of his hall, he showed us a cave and told us to walk inside and we'd meet the Dawnguard. We walked into the cave and after a few minutes walked out into what looked like a path. Turning right, we followed the path past the waterfalls on our right (south). Farther along the path, as the glade came into view and the path became more unforgiving, a buttress tower appeared. Continuing along the path, we came upon an Orc practicing his skills with a strange new weapon. He introduced himself as Durak. Following the path to the imposing fortress entrance, then entering the fortress. The Hall was huge with banners that were unfurled.

We each were given one of these strange new weapons. It was called Crossbow and (45) Steel Bolts. We were ready. I stopped for a minute to think when someone put his hand on my shoulder and asked what my thoughts were and I asked (without thinking) actually I wondered if shouts would work on a vampire and the guy said I could yell all I wanted but it properly wouldn't do much good. Heading into the initial cavern, I let out a loud yol toor followed by a yolshul turning every vampire to ash while everyone looked on in surprising awe.

At first, no one knew what to say other than Aela and Illia who both congratulated me on a good job but thought I should save it until next time for the big man/ monster. Moving on, the next room had a daemon in it. He said his name was Lord Harkon a true winged demonic Vampire Lord and aid to us that we "had" to choose. Throw our lot in with Lord Harkon and the Vampires or to refuse and continue to support the Dawnguard. I lowered my crossbow and took up my sword, "Wuuthrad" and swung it fiercely across the throat of this Lord saying, "This is my answer". What he didn't realize was that while I was lowering the crossbow and unsheathing the sword, I was stepping closer to the vampire lord and I literally chopped his head off. What we didn't figure on was that everyone Lord Harkon affected would eventually be cured. I then set his head and body on fire. The vampire wars were now over. The only thing left to do now was to find and destroy the Vampire that caused it all.

One of the three of us would not be coming back and would be missed greatly.

The Vampire mother was huge, half dragon, half something like a gargoyle. And she had a name "Durnehviir". I had to use Od ah viing just to see if it would work then To diin plus krii, then Paarthunard appeared breathing sheer fire onto the mother. Who died and whose soul came onto me. When I turned, I saw Illia kneel on the ground and it was Aela. I used heal other to Grand Healing which I drew upon my own soul to heal the one I truly loved in this world but as she became more powerful. I became less weak to give my life for another to live and as my eyes slowly closed, I heard a voice say, but the adventure isn't over yet and my eyes snapped open. I need to collect one more Dragon Soul, and then pass it on to Aela.

THE END

ABOUT THE AUTHOR

Ronald is a young man at heart who loves to play the Elder Scrolls series of games. He has been completely taken with the way that the stories evolve and the imagination of the storytellers. Ronald is also an avid lover of insects and their world. The innumerable species of each family just fascinates him. While Ron does love to read and play video games his greatest talent comes in his desire to create new and interesting things that people can use.